PAWN

NIGHT OF THE DARK FAE BOOK ONE

ANGELA J. FORD

Editing: Courtney Andersson of Elevation Editorial

Cover Design: Eerilyfair Book Covers

ISBN: 9781670763570

❀ Created with Vellum

A day will come when curses will be broken, the lost shall be found, the found shall be lost, and the rift between mortal and celestial will cease to exist

— PROPHECY OF ERINYES

CONTENTS

1

DUNGEON OF THE DAMNED

CHAINS RATTLED AGAINST IRON, and somewhere in the bleak darkness a banshee screamed. Its cry, like the sound of teeth grating against metal, high and wild, sent a shiver of trepidation down the spines of those who listened. A low growl echoed through the chambers, followed by a sharp bark. A sword slid into a warm body, the hilt sinking into fur and withdrawing with a slight sucking sound. Moans were soft, aware of the coming inevitable sentencing, and doom was near for those unlucky enough to be cast into the Dungeon of the Damned. Little light poured into the blighted prison, hidden far under the fertile earth of an island and crawling with the souls of the pure and the damned.

The newest prisoner, Maeve, knelt on the uneven stone floor, aware of the grime that now stained her bruised, bare knees. When she'd arrived at this godforsaken place, the fae—her jailers—had stripped away her breastplate, sword, shield, and crown. Upon her capture, a simple golden collar had been placed around her neck. Aside from the collar, she also wore a plain, sleeveless tunic that fell to her knees, leaving her long arms and legs bare to the elements. The tunic covered the pattern of brown ink that adorned her neck, chest, and upper arms. The patterns symbolized her heritage, a lost civilization, and even Maeve, the sole survivor of her people, did not know what they meant. The destruction of her homeland, Carn, had happened only twenty-five years ago, when Maeve was five or six, but when she tried to think back, memories of her people evaded her, lost like the cool winds of winter burned away in the warmth of sunlight.

Cold air crept into her windowless cell. Stale seawater dripped off the stones, creating a pool of stagnant liquid in the corner, her only source of refreshment. A putrid smell came from it, but she knelt all the same with her hands clasped in front of her. In between sips of water, she rocked back and forth, her mane of dark hair gracing her shoulders like a halo.

Maeve's lips moved as she whispered the same prayer she'd repeated every day since her imprisonment. She kept her steely blue eyes closed against the gloom, unwilling to let in the nightmarish images. Today marked her thirtieth day in the dungeon, and although the shrieks of the damned filled her with terror, she knew her time would come. She resolved to face judgement with the same determination that had carried her through every situation life had dealt her thus far.

Her capture was an accident, a fate no one could have saved her from. Not even him. The warlord she had fought and bled with. At the thought of him, she rocked faster. What had he thought when she did not appear after the raid? Did he see the jailers arrest her? And then there was the thought she pushed to the back of her mind, the desperate wish that she had not argued with him, that their last words had been on kinder terms. He would have known something was wrong when she did not show up, but would he assume it was because of their argument, not a situation out of her control? Unless . . . no. She did not want to think it, but the cold, damp, and loneliness pressed in, and she couldn't keep the horrific thought from invading her mind. Had he wanted the fae to take her and lock her away?

The jangling of keys grew louder until they were thrust in the lock of Maeve's cell. A bead of sweat trickled down her forehead and splashed onto a scarred stone. The muscles of her arms trembled as the eerie squeak of iron made her cringe. She remained in position, staring at the floor as the shadow fell over her.

"Get up," barked the rough voice of a jailer. "Hands behind your back. Don't try anything if you want to avoid the stocks."

Maeve took a deep breath, counting. They'd half-starved her and kept her locked up for thirty days, hoping to break her. But they hadn't, and the time had come to act. Another drop of sweat followed the path of the first and slid between her eyes to hang precariously on the edge of her nose. In one fluid motion, Maeve pushed off her heels and balanced on her hands, then swung her feet high over her head and slammed them into the neck of the jailer.

The assault took him by surprise and he fell with a shout. His hand fumbled for his belt as he stood, seeking the short metal rod with the glowing ember at the tip that burned the prisoners and brought them to submission, but Maeve was faster. She allowed her momentum to carry her through until she was back on her feet, upright. She kicked out at the jailer's thigh, then brought her knee up hard between his legs. He gave a muffled cry and collapsed to the floor again, holding his groin and swearing.

Keys clanged against the stones, but the jailer held them tight as he whimpered and then shouted, "Help! She's escaping! Catch her!"

Footsteps echoed off the walls. If she did not act quickly, she would be caught and locked up again.

Maeve placed her bare foot on the jailer's wrist and pressed down until his fingers came open and the keys fell free. Panic clawed up her throat as she bent to snatch them; they were warm and slippery from his sweaty hands. She made a face and leaped over the prone jailer just as a shock crackled through her right leg.

She spun, hair flying over one shoulder. The jailer sneered through his agony. He'd driven the rod into her calf, and a burning sensation had bolted across her skin like a hot knife being dragged up her leg. Gritting her teeth against the shriek in her throat, Maeve lashed out with the keys, dragging them across the jailer's face.

He screamed and dropped the rod as he pressed his hands against his cheek to stop the crimson flow that trickled down his chin.

Maeve darted out of the open cell, dragging her burning leg behind her. A whip slammed into her and ripped open the back of her shift with its teeth.

Maeve grunted and spun to face whoever had whipped her. Blood boiled under her skin and the familiar haze of battle lust rushed over her, dulling all pain while she fought.

The fae with the whip was too far away for her to strike. He leered, showing off a row of crooked yellow teeth. He was a slim creature, tall and skinny, who looked as though his bones would snap in half if stepped on. Unfortunately, she was familiar with him and knew he would bend, not break, if she fought him. The prisoners called him Nathair, the snake. His head was shaped like an adder's—flat, with gleaming yellow eyes that were more reptilian than fae. The row of yellow teeth in his mouth were sharp and pointy, and when his mouth was closed, the tips of his fangs hung out, completing his sinister look. Despite his scrawny appearance, he was fast and his whip acted as an extension of his arms. He lashed out again, and this time the whip curled around Maeve's arm that held the keys. The teeth of the whip sank into her skin. Her eyes narrowed, and she charged Nathair, determined not to release her chance at freedom.

The whip fell away, leaving angry red welts crisscrossing up her arm. Her free hand curled into a fist and she leaped into the air, drawing back her hand for maximum impact. The air gave her strength, but as she followed through with the strike, Nathair vanished.

A sinking sensation twisted through Maeve, but she was already airborne. She'd forgotten who she was fighting against and had failed to consider the tricks of the fae—namely, the ability to slip into the shadow world and reappear wherever they liked. Instantly.

A hand tipped her foot, and instead of flying, she crashed. She closed her eyes right before the impact and landed on her face. There was a snap and searing agony ripped through her nose as it broke. Warm liquid pooled from her face and her ears rang. She felt, rather than heard, the keys come free from her fingers and slide across the stone passage.

A sour odor hung in the air, and she realized it was her own vomit spilling from her lips. Her stomach convulsed again and again. Rough hands grabbed her, lifting and dragging her backward as she spit a mix of saliva and blood and bile.

Her mouth hung open, as the blood streaming from her nose made it difficult to breathe. She tilted her head back to stop the flow and gasped for air. A fist slammed into her ribs and tears sprang to her eyes. She bent over, coughing and hissing, but the jailers held her firm and pulled her back upright. Her arms were yanked behind her back and secured below the elbow with iron clamps, forcing her chest to thrust out awkwardly. She sucked in air through her parted lips while the jailers secured chains around her ankles, ignoring her pathetic struggles. Rage surged through her abused body and her stomach clenched as a jailer shoved her forward.

"Calm down, prisoner." Nathair's whispering tones made her shiver with revulsion. "You're to be taken to the Hall of Judgement."

Eyes wild, she tried to tilt her head to look at him, but a slow clap rang from the shadowed edge of the prison hall. Heat flared around her neck as the golden collar came alive, reacting to the sound of its master.

Maeve gulped for air as the heat cut off her breathing. Her vision went dizzy, yet still she pressed against the influence of the spell with all the strength she could muster.

"Feisty as expected; I told you not to transport her without me," a cold voice scolded the jailers.

Maeve sagged in her chains as the heat became unbearable, then evaporated.

"Master," hissed Nathair, clearly surprised. He recovered quickly. "You saw what she did. I ask leave to teach her a lesson with my whip."

"From the look of her, you've already begun," the Master snorted.

Nathair uttered an oath and curled up his whip.

The Master's cold voice faded as he walked away. "Bring her to the Hall of Judgement. I want her unspoiled. Ready to work."

2

HALL OF JUDGEMENT

"The accused shall kneel," the warden bellowed. He had the head of a bull with dark rough hair and curved horns, and although his hands were manlike, his feet were hooves. A heavy musk came from his animal-like body. A minotaur. A lesser one, but a fearsome enemy all the same. He stamped his javelin against the stone and pointed it at Maeve.

Maeve lifted her chin and drew up her shoulders as best she could with the heavy chains weighing her down. Her battle rage had faded, leaving her with a weary exhaustion. To compound her misery, the thin golden collar around her neck continued to drain her energy.

Two swift kicks to the back of her knees brought her crashing down, adding new scrapes to her old ones.

Keeping her chin raised in defiance, she glanced around the Hall of Judgement.

Thick black columns towered on either side, reaching to the inky blackness far above them. About ten feet over her head were yellow torches, the only light in the forsaken place. Jailers—some fae, others human—lined the hall, along with the court of the Master, made up of fae and beast alike. They had all come to witness and revel in the disgrace of their prisoners.

Memories flooded Maeve's mind, unhappy memories she'd long repressed. She'd assumed—wrongly—that the past lay behind her and a life of freedom was ahead of her. It had been a long time since she'd had a run-in with the fae, and to be back in their grasp was a blow to her pride. Strength was supposed to be her salvation—even though it was the fae who'd taught her how to use her abilities—but ultimately it had failed her. She closed her eyes, once again recalling the heat of flames and the searing pain as a blade drove into flesh over and over again. Screams and cries echoed in her mind, much like those she'd heard in her cell in the dungeon below.

A heady fragrance hung in the air, making Maeve's eyes water. She held back a sneeze to avoid doing any more damage to her broken nose. What she would give for a healer. Already, she could feel the swelling around her eyes. Squinting, she stared straight ahead into the darkness, which pointed like an arrow to the end of the hall, to the Dragon Throne. It was covered with bronze-colored dragon scales.

Some said that over five hundred years ago, the fae conquered the dragons, who had been intent on ruling the world. After destroying their civilization, the fae slew them all except the largest one, and used their black magic to force the last living dragon into an eternal slumber in the form of a throne. The intricate layers of the scales were so detailed, Maeve assumed the tale was true, but there was no possibility the dragon was still alive. For one, it did not have a head, and they would have had to kill it to force it to morph and shift into such an inert object. Because dragons had been slain hundreds of years ago, the tales about them often conflicted with each other, but everyone agreed that the race of dragons were dangerous, predatory, and untamable.

Maeve's vision swam. The Dragon Throne served as a reminder that she was in the home of monsters, the fae. Banished from the world above, they did not treat those who could walk in daylight kindly. There was no empathy in their hearts, only malice. Maeve suspected there was a bit of jealousy as well, though the fae could enter the world above during the night of the full moon, and that window of time was enough for them to carry out their wicked plans.

Maeve assumed, since they had brought her to the

Hall of Judgement, they were not interested in forcing her into servitude in the lightless kingdom or executing her. Which meant the Master wanted to make a deal with her. A deal she would have to take, for escape did not seem likely. Not with the pitiless gaze of the warden on her. She could hear the rattle in his chest as he growled, and his hooves clopped eerily as he circled her, like a wolf around a fawn.

Maeve swallowed hard. Did they sense her discomfort?

"Enough," the Master called out.

He stood by the Dragon Throne, a shadowy figure, intentionally hidden from the light. He towered well over six feet, yet kept his form shrouded in a velvety black cloak and his face hidden behind a black mask. Only his eyes were visible, and they were nothing more than liquid pools of darkness with no irises.

The gleam of his gaze met Maeve's, and she suppressed a shudder. He'd attacked her thirty days ago, during the full moon. She'd had a sick feeling in her stomach all day, as if her body was attempting to tell her something was wrong and that she should call off the raid. But she'd been headstrong, determined, and angry, and when the Master had appeared to capture her, she was taken off guard.

His fingers were long and slender. Sharp claws appeared on the edges and retracted, like those of a wildcat. Maeve recalled his claws sinking into the skin of her arm, the snarl on his face, and the hint of fangs as sharp as a wolf's. Then he'd collared and dragged her to his dungeon.

"Maeve of Carn." His sinister tone echoed off the stones. "I will not mince my words. Your actions and your crimes against the Divine drew our attention. You are a warrior, defender, and champion, and yet you forsook your sacred oath of protection. Because of your dark deeds and your particular skill set, we sought you out. We have decided you will fulfill a quest for us. Upon completion of the quest, I will grant you freedom."

Maeve's ears burned at his words. Crimes against the Divine? Dark deeds? He accused her and pointed the finger, but she was no champion, no protector of the people. The people of Carn were gone, dead. It was up to her to find her place in the world. Yet, her skill with the sword had landed her in a few hairy situations, and even though she worked as a mercenary seeking out the not-so-innocent and forcing them to face their crimes, she'd gotten careless. When faced with difficult situations, she'd let her battle rage overrule her judgement and acted with violence, killing those who should live, simply because they were in her way. Deep down, she knew her actions went against the laws of the Divine, but she'd assumed her deeds would not be judged in her lifetime. She clenched her jaw so hard it sent a spark of pain up the side of her face. "I'd rather rot than work for you," she spat, shaking with hatred.

A jailer lifted a hand and struck her across the face.

Maeve's head whipped back, jarring her broken nose. Pain blinded her and fresh blood spurted from her nostrils. She gagged as it blocked her throat and her chained fingers twisted, desperate to clear the fluid away.

After a moment, the sensation faded. When her vision cleared, she saw the Master had left his shadowed corner. His slippered feet kissed the stones as though he were gliding across a frozen lake. His lips parted, and she glimpsed his fangs poking out of the corners of his mouth.

"You have no choice," fury rolled through his words as he growled them. "This is a command. It is what you will do."

Maeve spit blood and examined her enemy. Her bruised lip curled. "Your offer is tempting, but how do I know you will keep your word?"

"Those who break rules do not get a choice," the Master rebuked her.

Heat flared up her neck, a reminder that he controlled her through the magical collar and she was nothing more than a slave to his commands.

"Listen well, Maeve of Carn. I alone can release you from the collar that holds you. I alone can reduce your sentence and let you go free. But I know your kind. You are full of self-righteousness and believe everything you do has an excuse, a reason. You forget the fundamental laws that shaped the world in the beginning of time, and you believe you can escape judgement for your deeds. You are wicked, but I see the merit in your skills. You hold a unique power, and although you are not fully human, you can walk among them. Unlike us, you need not hide from the sunlight. We have decided your redemptive path. You will return to the world where the humans dwell and find the Seven Shards of Erinyes. Every full moon, an agent of mine will meet you to bring the shards here."

Maeve froze, a dull horror beating inside her like the wings of a trapped bird. She opened her mouth, closed it, and opened it again. When her voice came out, it was only a whisper, and she stared up at the Master as though she'd heard wrong. "The Seven Shards of Erinyes? They have been lost for centuries . . ."

"Yes, and now to be found again. A scholar will assist in your quest. We have discovered the rough location of each shard. You will find them and bring them to me. Time is of the essence, but because of the perilous nature of this quest, we will give you seven months to complete it."

Maeve sputtered. Seven months? But it was a chance to return to daylight, walk among the humans again, and flee the rotting pit. Her mind worked through scenarios and possibilities. She'd redeem herself and find him. Seven months would give her time to find out how to free herself of the golden collar and thwart the plans of the Master.

When she looked up again, the Master stood within arm's length in a pool of torchlight. The paleness of his skin and the sharpness of his fangs made her quiver, but she faced him nonetheless. "If you would send me on this quest, I will need my weapons and my armor back."

He flicked his fingers. "We have arranged it."

Maeve took a deep breath as boldness came over her. "You have collared me, which reduces my strength. If you would have me succeed in recovering the shards, I will need access to my full abilities."

The black pools of his eyes became deeper, and the Master bent over, bringing his face far too close to hers. Maeve wanted to shrink away from the scents of blood and decay that surrounded him. There was a sharp click as his claws extended, and he placed them under her chin. His aura surrounded her, and she felt as though she'd been dunked into a pool of darkness and it was him, and only him, that she could see.

When he spoke, his voice echoed both inside and outside of her head, ripping through all her private thoughts and shredding them. "Do you know why they call me the Master? I have seen civilizations rise and fall, and you are but a means to an end. Your power is mine, and until I see fit, you will wear the collar. If you think you can blindside me, betray me, and escape, think again. You have a fire in your soul, but I am the king of the fae. I can send you to eternal misery if you even think about disobeying me. I can make everyone and everything you care about suffer, and I can bend your will to servitude. That flash of defiance in your spirit will help you find the shards, but if you turn it against me, I will release the Underworld's fury on you. Now go—and remember, you wear my mark. Wherever you go, whatever you do, I will find you. If you haven't retrieved all seven shards within seven months, your life will be forfeit."

3

ISLE OF DARKNESS

SUNLIGHT KISSED Maeve's face as the portal spit her out on the island. She squinted against the light and waited, allowing her eyes to adjust to the brilliance. Despite the dark mission hanging over her, the fresh scent of salt-infused waves and the warmth from the sun gave a buoyancy to her attitude.

The fae, keen to stay away from the sunlight, had sent her through a portal instead of allowing her to use the tunnels to access the Isle of Darkness, the gateway to the fae's Underground. On the island, crumbling, sand-bleached towers had given way to overgrown grass and the occasional tree, and four statues, each standing over fifty feet high, supported each corner of the watchtower. The statue that looked north was headless, with long robes and a broken sword in his, or her, hands. The one that looked south was an angel with one wing; the other had been shattered. She looked fierce as she gazed, sightless, across the shore. The ones that looked east and west each had one hand bearing a javelin outstretched, as if preparing to throw it at those who dared attempt entering the Underground.

Maeve stood on the watchtower lookout, which allowed her to see down the cliffs to the sea, where wild waves splashed up at the shoreline, chipping away at the ragged stairs that led down. To her right, on a crumbling staircase, sat a human woman. At least, she looked human. She appeared middle-aged with strands of silver in her dark hair, which was piled in a bun at the base of her neck. She had an ageless, elegant beauty, and once might have been a noblewoman, though wrinkles now surrounded her gray eyes, which had a sad droop to them. She wore a simple black robe and gloves, and a bundle sat by her feet. In her lap was a book. She frowned, and her voice came out hard and clipped. "You must be Maeve."

"I am." Maeve narrowed her eyes. "Who are you?"

"Didn't they tell you?" she muttered darkly, glancing at the statues and down her nose at the sea. "I'm Sandrine. The scholar."

Maeve stared and almost laughed. "You? The scholar? I thought they would send a warrior."

Sandrine snorted. "One is enough. They don't want us getting any ideas."

Maeve chewed her lip and glanced out toward the horizon. It was midday, perhaps later. If they started now, they could reach the shoreline before midnight. "That means you know where we are going?"

Sandrine drew her thin shoulders up defensively. "I would not be going with you if I did not know where to go," she snapped.

Maeve held out a hand, frustration mounting. "I did not mean to offend you. This is just irregular and unexpected."

Sandrine sniffed. "Irregular? Unexpected? Where do you think we are?"

Maeve had to admit she had a point.

"Are you going to stand there while the sun sets, or will you gather your things?" Sandrine snapped her book shut and pointed to a second bundle that Maeve had missed.

Maeve's eyes widened, and she dashed forward, giving a grunt of pain as the wounds on her face and arms protested her movements. There was her sword, tucked into its scabbard with the leather belt wound around it as though to protect it. The familiar weight felt good. One hand went around the hilt, holding the familiar fibers and the grip that had given her the calluses on her palms. Her hands had gone soft in the past thirty days, and she hugged it closer, her fingers molding to the familiar dips and ridges. Her hand clenched, and a ripple of anger passed through her, slight and small, just a hint of what she would do when she was free to fight as she wished.

She frowned, aware of Sandrine watching her.

Maeve considered unsheathing her sword and striking the frail woman dead on the spot, then running as fast and as far as she could before the Master and the jailers caught up with her. With a sigh, she dismissed the thought. She was determined to turn over a new leaf. No more killing, harming of innocents, trickery, or betrayal. That dark life was over; if she wanted to escape the fae, she needed to change.

She began pulling on her armor. A breastplate, gauntlets for her arms and legs, and her leather sandals with crisscross straps that went up to her knees. Finally, she lifted her crown with its ruby stone. She held it for a moment, and her eyes misted over. Queen of nothing. The ruby crown, her birthright, had been passed from generation to generation—until an earthquake and a war wiped out the people of Carn, leaving Maeve to scramble from one hired job as a warrior to the next. As much as she hated to admit it, the Master was right. She'd committed many sins. Until now.

She slipped the crown onto her forehead and felt the warmth of the ruby. Her eyes flickered to Sandrine, who watched her with a critical eye.

Maeve buckled her sword onto her back and picked up her copper shield. If nothing else, she should be nice to the scholar. Someone wise to the world could turn into a powerful ally, unless the fae were holding something over her head. "Why were you in the Dungeon of the Damned?" she asked, as a way of making conversation and finding out more about her companion.

"You mean, what did I do? They captured me for murdering my husband. I was faithful and gave the bastard nine children, and then he cast me out, exchanging me for some whore half his age. Why should he have happiness when he made me miserable? I killed him for it. I'm not sorry, so they are forcing me to join you, which is punishment enough. I'd rather rot in the Dungeon of the Damned than be forced to travel with the likes of you." She sniffed.

Maeve's attitude soured. She'd have to work twice as hard to gain Sandrine as an ally, for the woman seemed determined to keep Maeve at a distance.

Squaring her shoulders, she faced the sea. The crumbling staircase ran down almost to the water, and tied to a protruding stone was a boat. Maeve pointed. "Is that for us?"

Sandrine put away her book, threw her bundle over her back, and started down the staircase. "If you want to make the shore before midnight, we should leave now. I hope you have some strength in those arms to row."

Maeve frowned and followed. "Is this the sea I think it is?"

Sandrine gave a humph. "The Sea of Sorrows. Best to be away as soon as possible, before the shadow people take your sanity."

Maeve groaned and touched her face. Even though the fae had allowed her to clean the blood, it was still tender to the touch. The skin around her nose was puffy, and a dull pain thudded in the back of her skull. "When we reach land, I need a healer. Will you find one en route to the first shard?"

"I thought you'd never ask," Sandrine said. "When we get to the bottom, I will fix your broken nose. I assume you don't have any other complaints?"

"You're a healer too?"

"I dabble," Sandrine said, but there was a lighter lilt to her tone of voice.

Maeve did not respond, although she was relieved to realize the Divine was with her. Part of her prayers had been answered. Now they just needed to navigate the Sea of Sorrows before the shadow people attacked.

The Sea of Sorrows was named for spirits who had lost loved ones and desired revenge. Instead of passing to the afterlife, they clung to their former lives and became half-alive; shadow people. They sought to take over the bodies of the living so they could enact revenge on those who had caused them misery. The fae had made their home underneath the island on the Sea of Sorrows to dissuade the living from visiting them. Only the desperate would navigate this sea, and often only with a powerful spell to keep them from being drowned by the spirits.

Maeve hoped the fae had seen fit to spell the boat that bobbed in the water. She was unsure how true the rumors about the Sea of Sorrows were, and she did not want to find out.

They continued down the old staircase, Maeve following behind Sandrine until they reached solid ground. The beach was sandy, and grit sunk between Maeve's toes. She eyed the sea with a growing sensation of discontent. Legend said that even a drop of water against bare skin was enough to send a vision of madness into one's mind.

"Come," Sandrine commanded, dropping her bag into the sand.

Maeve moved to stand in front of the shorter woman.

"Kneel." Sandrine pointed to the sand, her words ringing out with a strange power odd for someone so small.

Reluctantly, Maeve buried her sore knees in the sand. It caked on her skin, sinking into her pores and making her itch.

"Close your eyes. This will hurt," Sandrine said.

Maeve obeyed.

Sandrine's fingers touched the tender part of her nose. A slight pressure built until it became uncomfortable to breathe. Maeve willed herself to stay in place as the throbbing increased to a crescendo, and then just as suddenly melted away.

"That's better," Sandrine said, wiping her hands on her robe.

She picked up two oars and passed them to Maeve. "You'd better take these. I will navigate, but brute strength is your gift."

Maeve took them, slightly insulted by being called a brute. Gingerly, Maeve touched her face. The swelling had gone down and there was no pain. "Thank you," she said begrudgingly, and climbed into the boat.

It was a mere fishing boat, narrow and low to the ground, with a space in the bottom for their bundles and a plank of wood for each to sit on. Maeve dipped the oars into the water and planted her feet firmly on the bottom of the boat.

Sandrine sat down and leaned over to saw off the rope. It separated with a snap, and the vessel sank an inch or two. Using the oars, Maeve pushed away from the shore. The boat slid off easily, moving into the waves with surprising grace.

Maeve glanced down at the shimmering waters, and just beneath the surface she saw shadows glide by. The shape of a body coalesced and Maeve ripped her gaze away, focused on the horizon, and rowed as fast as she dared.

4

SEA OF SORROWS

MAEVE PULLED hard on the oars as her gaze focused on the low clouds gathering on the horizon. A storm brewed, and the air smelled like salt. Maeve licked her lips and wished the fae had given them a boat with a sail. The wind would blow them to shore much faster than she could row, especially given her limited strength. She settled into a rhythm, her breath coming short and fast, muscles rippling. Every now and again she glanced over at her strange companion, Sandrine.

The scholar held a pouch in her hands, and her fingers shook as she undid the knots. Her straightforward, brusque manner was still there, but her wrinkled face was pale.

Maeve followed her gaze. The shadow under the water swam closer, the inky dark splotch taking the shape of a human. Nay. Not a human. An angry soul.

Maeve tried to steady her breathing as coal-black eyes stared out of the water, glaring at her. Anger rippled across the surface, and Maeve's skin crawled as the sensation of fury came over her. She picked up her speed, but the shadow stayed with them, matching her strokes. Then a hand, pure obsidian, reached out to touch the hull of the boat and tip it over.

Sandrine's body jerked as she hurled a black substance at it.

The shadow gave a hiss and the hand dipped back into the waters.

Maeve puffed and panted. "What was that? Salt?"

Sandrine patted her bag. "Pepper," she grunted. "Salt would do no good. You are aware we are in the sea, which is made of salt? It would only encourage the shadow people."

Maeve nodded, ignoring the smugness in Sandrine's words. "How did you know it would drive them away?"

Sandrine pinched the bridge of her nose and huffed. "I'm a scholar. Are you done with stupid questions?"

Maeve pressed her lips together and threw her frustration into rowing. But it wasn't enough. The words buzzed on her lips, begging to be said out loud. She gave in, and through gritted teeth, growled, "You don't have to be unpleasant. We're stuck on this quest together without a choice. We don't have to be friends, but we can at least be amicable."

Sandrine snorted but said nothing else, keeping her gaze on the water.

Time dragged onward slowly. Maeve glanced again toward the horizon as the sun sank, casting a rainbow of radiance across the sky. Shadows trailed their boat, although the shadow people did not come closer. The wind began to whip up, shaking the waters and casting the waves higher.

Sandrine remained a hostile companion, her gaze straight ahead. "It should be here soon. Any moment now."

"Land?" Maeve gasped out. The speed she was rowing at strained her muscles, and her strength was fading into exhaustion. Curses came to mind as she thought of the Master, who had tampered with her strength. Without the golden collar, she could have rowed just as fast for twice as long without growing weary. Was this how humans felt all the time?

The last glimmer of light vanished and Maeve's senses heightened. The smack of the oars moving in and out of the water made her shiver. The wind caused goosebumps to pimple on her bare skin, and a flash of purple lightning lit up the sky, showing Maeve her companion.

Sandrine stood up, making the boat rock back and forth, and pointed with a crooked finger. She looked like a wild witch as the wind pulled her silver-streaked hair free from her bun and the brief flash of light made her eye sockets appear hollow. "There!" Sandrine's voice rang with triumph.

Maeve whipped her head around just as another strike lit up the sky. She saw craggy towers, sharp and wicked in the storm. Land. Shelter. The sight renewed her vigor, and she reached deep down into her core to pull the last strands of strength she needed. Her arms shook from the effort and her bottom was sore and numb from sitting so long on the wooden plank.

The boat shot forward, responding as though Maeve had spoken aloud to it. She closed her eyes and pulled with all her might just as a horrific clap of thunder vibrated through the waters and a cloud burst. A torrent of rain poured out of the night sky as though she had just rowed under the thunderous might of a waterfall.

The boat tipped precariously to one side, and the strength of the rain knocked an oar free from Maeve's hand. Uttering a cry, she reached out, her fingers snatching at nothing but cold air and furious rain.

Fingers cold as death wrapped around her wrist and tugged. Before Maeve could react, memories invaded her mind, but not her memories—someone else's.

She saw a child, a little boy or girl—she couldn't tell with the shaved head—but the child was no more than a few years old. A strength gripped her, a desperate desire to do anything to save the child. Two people held her arms back, and she fought, kicking, biting, and scratching. Reaching the child was of the utmost importance. It was a matter of life and death. Fury engulfed her and burned like a raging fire as the strangers dragged the screaming child farther and farther away. And then she was free.

Picking up a stick, she beat those who'd held her back, once, twice, thrice, then raced after those carrying away the child. Her precious child, who she'd carried in her swollen womb for nine months and birthed after long hours of agony and pain. When she'd finally held the wailing child at her breast, a fierce joy had overwhelmed her, forcing her to sob and hold the babe close, swearing nothing would happen to it. And nothing had —until now. Until warriors invaded, destroyed her village, and killed her husband. The child was all she had left. She would not lose it.

A bonfire lit up the shadows around her. Men ran, women screamed, and children wailed. Sword and shield clanged together, but she bolted through them. Her own life was not worth saving, but she'd gladly die a thousand deaths to save the child. When she reached the ones who had taken her child, their wicked knives glittered in the light and pointed first at her and then the child.

A horrible rushing came to her head, and she screamed with all her might as they drove the blade in over and over again. She was too late. Tears streamed down her face and she beat her breast, wailing in misery.

Desperate to avenge her child, she snatched up a burning branch and ran toward them. Something went through her, and in an instant, her body went cold. So cold. Her limbs. She could not feel them. Oh, Divine One. She could not move them at all. And then there was the child, her lost child. She needed revenge. They had to pay . . .

Something slapped her across her face and Maeve gasped, limbs flailing as she came out of the vision.

"Maeve! Fool girl, wake up and swim."

Pepper filled the air, and she coughed, thinking she might have swallowed some along with the salt water. Her insides burned and the rain would not cease. Purple lightning showed her Sandrine's white face. She was bobbing in the water and lifting her hand to slap Maeve again.

"Wait, no. I'm here," Maeve protested.

"Swim," Sandrine shouted. "They will return!"

5

BAY OF BISCANE

THE FULL MOON shone down on the beach as Maeve and Sandrine hauled themselves out of the ocean, gagging and spitting out mouthfuls of foul water. Vivid hatred still plagued Maeve's mind. She could not forget the vision of the woman, nor the child, stabbed before she could save it. Her limbs trembled. She tried to recall the men's faces. They had to pay for what they had done.

"Don't dwell on it. Whatever you saw." Sandrine knelt in the sand, sweeping strands of wet hair back into a bun. The moonlight revealed the quaver of her chin, although her gray eyes were cold.

Maeve rose to her feet, checking to ensure her weapons and armor were all intact. "It felt real," she whispered. "The woman. The child. The soldiers. It was awful. I never considered how someone else might feel. The victims."

"Because it was real," Sandrine said. "The memories you . . . *we* saw were real. They happened to people like you and I. The only difference is, they also lost their lives. Terrible things happen in this world, and people like you can stop them if you stop focusing on quests that are self-serving."

The words burned, turning into fury as Maeve absorbed them, and then dust. Sandrine thought her selfish, consumed with her own self-serving interests. Her rebuttal died on her lips. It was true. Ever since she'd become a hired warrior—at times a bounty hunter—her actions had been selfish. She never considered whether her victims were innocent; instead she had focused on catching and turning them over for a pouch of gold. There was the father who had stolen a crate of goods from a merchant. She'd hunted him down and struck down the sons who tried to fight her when she'd captured the man. He'd wept, pleading his innocence, but she'd turned him over regardless. Then there was the thief in the citadel, hunted by the king's men. The thief had a camp of men, women, and children in a nearby forest. Maeve had joined the warriors who hunted the thief and turned him over to the king's guard to have his hands cut off for pillaging the kingdom. Those in his camp were imprisoned, perhaps executed, but Maeve had left with her bag of gold before finding out what happened to them. And the woman who had lived in a cave near the coast. She was a warrior, and had often stopped merchants who traveled along the coast, stealing their wares. Maeve had killed her, but before she died she begged for mercy. She did not want to leave her children alone, on their own. Maeve, who had never seen any children with the woman, hadn't believed her, and hadn't cared . . . but what if she had been wrong about each of those people? What if they had been innocent? What if they hadn't deserved the fate she'd doomed them to?

Her reflections returned to her argument with the warlord, Caspian, she had served until the night of the full moon. A familiar panicky sensation rose in her at the thought of him. Initially, she had thought he was like every other warlord, hardened and stubborn, desensitized from fighting the wars of others, claiming land, and stockpiling wealth. Their initial meeting was in the dueling ring. Maeve was between jobs and her coin was running out, so she'd resorted to dueling. The dueling rings were ugly, full of brutes and bloodthirsty crowds. Maeve had taken a beating more than once, but none could match her strength, and dueling often opened doors to more work for her. As it did with Caspian, who took note and invited her to join his warriors on their next task. It had gone well, and she'd worked for him ever since. However, things changed.

Six months ago, Caspian decided his warriors would stop fighting and thieving for the sake of wealth, and would instead aim for something greater, something noble. Maeve blamed the change on his visits to temples. He'd studied with a priest and priestess of the

Divine. While he refused to take on vows, he sought to understand the deeper meaning of life, and he'd become enlightened to the struggles of the people around him and his unique ability to offer solace and release from the difficulties and sorrows humans cast on each other.

Maeve was unhappy with the way he'd changed, and so quickly. It wasn't that she did not want to help people, it simply seemed impossible for one warrior to make much of an impact, if at all. There were so many people in the world with power: kings, warlords, mages, priests, slavers, and the fae—just to name a few—plus the creatures, like orcs, who preyed on small villages. Caspian insisted that the way warriors and warlords treated the lives of others was not in line with the way of the Divine. Killing just to kill and killing for wealth was a sort of darkness. It wasn't that Maeve did not believe him—after all, she prayed to the Divine, when she had a need. But Caspian claimed there was more.

Now, as Maeve stood on the shore and listened to Sandrine's words, she understood on a deeper level what Caspian had tried to share with her. The memory hung, trapped in her thoughts, and she wondered how many lives she'd unknowingly shattered with her actions. Actions that had led her down an immoral path and into the hands of the fae.

"Where are we?" she asked to avoid the pricking of her conscious.

"The Bay of Biscane."

Biscane. The word sounded familiar.

Sandrine continued. "Biscane is known for the warlords who keep towers full of wealth on the island, away from the mainland. We've landed on the northern end, which means we should be unseen. The law of truce applies here; everyone minds their own business, and trading takes place in the Village of the Lawless on the northeastern side of the bay."

It dawned on Maeve why the name sounded familiar. Caspian had a tower, a refuge, on the southern end of Biscane, closer to the mainland and the citadel. During the year they'd spent running from battle to battle, he'd mentioned it, but she'd never been there. He often sent his comrades off to store treasure there, though, and they had a hired a ship to take the riches across the King's Sea to his fortress. Maeve had been on the northeastern end of Biscane, to the outpost, also known as the Village of the Lawless. It was a haven for outcasts and warriors, a place to hide out, spend coin, or look for work.

She gazed at the wicked towers, glimmering like rows of knives in the white moonlight. Another full moon. She shivered, wondering if the fae were out, watching her progress.

A sudden hope beat in her breast. Would he be home? Lying low? Could she find him, seek refuge, and ask forgiveness for her bullheadedness? She fingered the golden collar around her neck, debating whether she'd tell him about her fate.

"We shall head toward one of the towers farthest from the outpost. A retired warlord, Lord Sebastian, dwells there, and you will find the first shard in his treasury," Sandrine said.

Maeve scratched her head. The fae expected her and a worn-out scholar to perform a heist in the middle of a highly protected bay, near an outpost where the only escape would be to dive into the Sea of Sorrows or—if they could make it to the eastern side—the Sea of Eels. "We will be caught," she frowned. "I don't understand how the fae expect us to penetrate a fortress on an island full of warriors. This is not my first choice. Do you have any ideas?"

Sandrine raised an eyebrow. Maeve thought if she were taller, she'd look down her nose at Maeve.

"Sleep and a full belly should give you some ideas." Sandrine jerked her chin north. "See the outcropping of rocks? There should be a cave where we can rest and hide for the remainder of the night."

Maeve shivered and rubbed her hands over her arms. Salt sloughed away from her skin. What she would give for a hot fire and a warm bowl of soup.

"It would be foolish to start a fire," Sandrine said, as though reading her mind. "The shores are guarded, and anyone who found us would not be kind to people who came out of the Sea of Sorrows."

Maeve nodded, aware that Sandrine spoke the truth.

Using the moonlight, they made their way up the sandy beach and around jagged rocks to the cliffs that shot out over the bay. Caves loomed like eyeless sockets, providing shelter from the bitter rain and the relentless waves. Maeve trudged with her head down, considering her unique predicament. She would not survive if she were caught hunting for shards in the Bay of Biscane. It was protected on three sides by water, and the fortresses kept the fourth side fortified against those who wished to devour the wealth of Biscane.

Not every tower in the bay was kept by retired warlords; there were plenty that manned ships and went forth to conquer villages and towns. Some were brave enough to weather the storms of the ocean and travel to the far north, while most went south.

After a few minutes, Sandrine found a shallow cave for them to rest in for the night. Without a word to Maeve, she stretched out on the hard rock with her bundle, as though she were not cold and drenched from their swim in the sea. Maeve bit her lip and resigned herself to a light sleep, waking fitfully as the waves crashed against rocks. When deep sleep claimed her, she dreamed of the woman and the child. Low moans and desperate cries echoed throughout her slumber.

6

WIZARD'S TOWER

A CLOUD of smoke bloomed above Imer's dark head, then caught the wind, which carried it up and across the battlements and into the serene blue sky. A sigh of satisfaction passed from his lips, along with another cloud of the semi-gray smoke. The rich smell of herbs and leather—a strange combination—passed under his nose, and he took a long whiff of the tobacco, drawing it into his lips and releasing it with his nostrils.

"Take it easy with the smoking, Imer," drawled a lazy—and slightly slurred—voice. "We have to leave in the morning."

One corner of Imer's mouth tugged up, and he rested his head against the stone wall of the tower, closing his eyes. "Aye, so ye say when you're drunker than a bamboozled wretch."

"Drunker than a man on his wedding night," the other voice snorted.

Opening his eyes, Imer raised an eyebrow. His brother, Ingram, sat across from him, his back propped up against the wall, legs spread, and a bottle of Fire's Breath in one hand. Ingram had coaxed the tavern keeper into handing the bottle of rum over for free. Ingram had a way with words, and his silver tongue and one eye often encouraged others to take some sort of pity on him. Pity he did not need.

Imer grinned at memories of how they'd duped others—all in good fun, though. Their last mischievous joke had landed them a bag of coins, which Imer had used to hire a tailor. He sat up straighter, admiring his new clothes. Imer and his brother were both dressed from head to toe in rich, elegant black clothes lined with red around the edges. Usually they wore hats to cover their features, which gave them away for who they were. Sticking to the shadows and blending in was the reason they were still alive. Although they called the wizard's tower home, they never stayed for more than a few months at a time. There were three homes they roamed between, returning to safety now and again when the direness of their situation forced them to seek haven.

"Master Ingram! Master Imer!" a panicked voice called from below.

"Bah," Ingram moaned, "can't they leave us alone?

One last night in safety to celebrate, and still the orders come."

Imer took the pipe from his mouth and frowned, his ears picking up the sound of running. "It's the lad, Jordan."

"Jordan the messenger, all he brings is bad news."

Imer grinned at his brother's mopey demeanor. "Perhaps it is good news this time."

Ingram took another long swig of his drink before tossing the empty bottle over the edge of the battlement. He raised a dirty finger, partly covered with his gloves. "I wager it's bad news. I'll give you ten coins if it's good."

A crash sounded from below as the bottle shattered on the cobblestones. There was a cry and then the squawk of a chicken.

Imer snorted. "If you had coin to wager, I'd take you up on it, but I'm fairly certain you spent it all on drink."

"I'm fairly sure you spent yours all on smoke," Ingram returned.

"Hardly fair," Imer protested, standing and patting his chest. "Look at our fine clothes, and the new feathers for our hats. I spent our coin on a worthy cause!"

"Master Ingram! Master Imer!" A lad dashed up the stairs, his short curly black hair wet with sweat and his long arms and legs pumping. He slowed down when he saw them, and relief crossed his brown face. "The wizard requests an audience with you. Before you depart," he blurted out.

Imer stared at the lad. What pompous words from a youth. The wizard requested nothing. He made demands in exchange for protection, and those who sought shelter at the wizard's tower obeyed his every word. Otherwise . . .

Imer shuddered when he remembered how it had been for him and Ingram before they found the wizard's tower. Perched in a hidden corner of the known land, the tower was a city in itself, albeit a small one. The tower was surrounded by a high stone wall, and within the wall were the workers, those who lived under the shadow of the wizard, seeking protection while earning a living. On the outskirts of the area was grazing land for the flocks they kept, a place to plant gardens, and a place for the warriors to practice. They had a bakery, a blacksmith, a winery, livestock—chickens, cows, pigs, goats—and messengers who gathered knowledge from the world at large.

Imer shook his head to organize his thoughts. He and his brother had unique abilities. Others saw them as odd, or wanted to use them for their skill. After his experiences in the wider world, he knew it was better to trade service for protection within the hidden wizard's tower, a haven for mages. True, the mages of the wizard's tower had problems and politics of their own, but mostly, it was a welcome respite. When they grew antsy, the wizard sent them out on quests, usually to quiet unrest and keep chaos from coming to the tower's doorstep. It was astonishing how wild the world was with corruption, but it was more than that. Rumor had it the fae were taking people, and the actions of the fae would make the Prophecy of Erinyes come true. The wizard claimed that it was in everyone's best interest for the Prophecy of Erinyes to come true, and whatever they could do to speed it along would help.

Imer stretched in an attempt to sharpen his mind, then peered over the battlements, taking in deep breaths of the late summer air. The view from the top of the tower was nothing short of glorious. To the south lay a great body of water sparkling in the distance, while to the north was the mountain that hid the tower's presence. It was difficult to access the tower, and the mists that hid it from view and the way it blended in with its surroundings made it even more so. Indeed, finding the wizard's tower was nigh impossible—unless one had magic.

Flexing his fingers, Imer took one last deep breath, then tucked the pipe away. "Lead on then, Jordan, we're coming."

The inside of the tower smelled like books, old parchment, scrolls, candles, and wax. The battlements were halfway up, the best place for warriors to station themselves should the wizard's tower ever come under attack. Inside though, winding staircases led all the way up to where the wizard held audience and kept his magic.

The first time Imer had entered the wizard's domain, he'd been mute with astonishment. Thousands of scrolls covered the walls, the books in the library were thick tomes full of secrets, and the uncanny scent of wisdom somehow filled the air. It was enough to breathe in the same air as the legends had and know he was in the presence of something much greater than himself. When he stood at the top of the wizard's tower, he understood the pull toward the sky, the move heavenward, and the desire to awaken the celestials and bring them back down to the land. Then, and only then, would there be an end to their suffering. No longer would they be hunted, and humans would not see them as oddities for use. Instead, they would see them for what they were: magnificent beings, full of old power, like the celestials.

A shiver of excitement went through him. He reveled in that, and in the knowledge that his actions would cause such drastic, life-changing events. By the Divine, if their efforts played a part in waking the legendary celestials, it would all be worth it.

Jordan, a young lad with entirely too much energy for the late afternoon, dashed ahead of them up the winding stairs, past golden banners and tomes collecting dust. When they reached the upper atrium with the arched doorways and wide windows letting light stream in, Jordan came to a stop. He swung his brown arms and legs in a wide gesture, pointing toward the doors, then bowed and scurried away. Likely to continue on with his next message. He was a runner—the fastest Imer had ever seen—but other than being quick of foot and fast with memory, Imer had seen no other manifestations of the boy's abilities.

As soon as Jordan disappeared, the door to the inner chamber opened. A woman walked out, her hips swaying as she strode toward them. In one hand she held a long, unsheathed blade that caught the sunlight. She was dressed in simple garb: a short halter that left her belly bare and a long skirt that settled low on her hips, revealing even more flesh. Willow. Imer gave her a wolfish grin which, to her credit, she ignored.

"Don't take up too much of his time," she said in passing. She smelled like magic, raw and dangerous, and there was a wicked glint in her amethyst eyes.

She brushed up against Ingram and then turned around, pausing her departure. He gave her a cool, aloof appraisal, his usual distant greeting. Ingram had a stand-offish approach, while Imer preferred to flirt. It was more fun that way.

Her perfect nose wrinkled. "Are you drunk?" she asked, her eyes narrowing in disdain at Ingram.

Imer laughed, both at her disdain and the disgruntled look on Ingram's face. Ingram had the allure, the ability to pull people toward him, and most woman ignored Imer and fell in love with Ingram's hardened, stony demeanor. Not that Imer minded, he got in enough trouble as it was, but Ingram often had to deal with love-languished women following him around, and they often lost their wits after he bedded them. It was best to stay away from womenfolk, no matter how desirable and attractive they were. Besides, Willow spent so much time with the wizard, Imer knew she aimed to become the next wizard of the tower. There was a cold ruthlessness hidden under her beauty.

Ingram growled. "Are you judging how I celebrate?"

Willow took a step back and smiled sweetly at him. "Just insulted you did not invite me."

Ingram tilted his head back, studying Willow, then shrugged. "Find me later . . ." he said, but there was no promise in those words, mere jest.

Willow frowned, crossed her arms over her chest, then turned and walked away, her hips swaying from side to side. Ingram stared after her until Imer punched his shoulder. "Careful brother, you still have a priestess waiting for you in Isdrine."

"I haven't forgotten," Ingram returned, his voice low. "But don't you wonder . . ."

Imer sped up so he wouldn't hear his brother's words. Wonder. Of course he wondered what Willow knew. But getting her drunk and seducing her wouldn't be the best way to find out. He shot a side glance at his brother before they both stepped into the domain of the wizard.

Multi-colored prisms covered the hall, creating a myriad of colors so rich it was almost impossible not to cover one's eyes. In a moment, the flare of magic died away, and the wizard appeared, blowing on his wand.

Imer paused just inside the doorway, heart pounding as he crossed his arms over his chest and waited.

The wizard glanced at them and then strode over, his robes billowing out behind him. He was not a traditional wizard. Although he was old—in years—his hair was black instead of white, he did not possess a beard, and he had the spryness of a man in his youth. It was his eyes, deep and magnetic, that gave away who he was.

"Ingram. Imer," he said. His words came out rushed, as though he were short of breath. "The hunter has risen."

The rest of the wizard's words were lost as a sudden ringing came to Imer's ears. His blood ran cold, and for a moment he wondered if they should leave the wizard's tower after all.

7

SEVEN SHARDS

"TELL ME ABOUT THE SEVEN SHARDS," Maeve asked Sandrine the next morning.

There was nothing to eat as Maeve and Sandrine walked north among the rocks, though Sandrine said after midday the waters would be clean enough to fish from, or they could search the rocks for crustaceans.

Maeve wondered how Sandrine knew so much, but the scholar did not seem ready to talk about herself any more than she already had, and Maeve was growing tired of her pointed remarks.

"Ah. The seven shards," Sandrine's dry voice gentled with wonder. "Legend says thousands of years ago, before the angels fell from the Divine's grace, they lived above the world as celestial beings and worshipped the Divine in an everlasting paradise. The scrolls state that the souls of the righteous rest with the

Divine after death, although you need to visit a temple and speak with a priest or priestess to find the path of righteousness. Once you gain access to the heavenly kingdom of the Divine, wealth and wisdom are yours for an eternity, and those you lost in life will be with you, forever and always. That is a promise of the Divine.

"However, the angels, beings sworn to worship and protect the Divine, stole a relic from the Divine's treasury. It was a crown made of seven crystals with a bluish aura to them. When the Divine discovered the theft, there was a war among the celestials. Half were cast down to the Underworld, not to be mistaken with the fae's Underground. They are now called demons, and they seek to undo all that the Divine built as vengeance for being kicked out of everlasting paradise. It is said the Divine was not unkind, and he gave the demons many chances to repent, but they were headstrong and determined to become more than they ought to have been, to become divine creatures who ruled the souls of all. They walk the earth as they are able, seeking to corrupt humankind, darken souls, and drag all down to the Underworld, where everlasting torment awaits as punishment for their deeds. After the war, the crown was cast down by the Divine. When it fell to earth, the seven shards were scattered across our known world, and most of the relic's power was lost. But not all of it. Legend says, if one can find all seven shards and put them back together into a crown, the reconstructed artifact will have the power to break all curses simultaneously."

Maeve listened, her forehead furrowing at the story. She believed some of it, but other parts seemed outlandish, impossible. But the people of Carn were not human, and they boasted extraordinary powers—perhaps the powers of fallen angels? She was unsure, for that part of her heritage was missing. Dwelling on the past brought her no joy, and there was no reason to question what had happened to Carn. The land was in ruins, taken over by the orcs. She frowned, hoping one of the shards wasn't there, too.

"Why do the fae want the shards?" she asked, curious to hear Sandrine's speculation.

Sandrine's sharp gray eyes met hers. "You caught the fae's attention, which means you must be a warrior exalted above all others, but you'd be a fool not to see what they intend. The fae have been banished from the earth, and although they walk it every full moon, they want more. You've seen what they can do, and you've likely heard the legend of the Dragon Throne. What more could they do if they were free from the curse?"

Maeve's fingers touched the golden collar, which hung loosely around her neck. Its touch burned against her skin, and again the words came to her. *The power to break all curses.* If she had the seven shards, she could free herself. Yet, just the memory of the dark eyes of the Master made her go cold. He was also aware of that fact, and he must have known her thoughts would drift to double-crossing him. That's why she had seven months. The fae would cast a portal, come to her, and take the pieces one by one. She'd never find all seven shards before they were taken from her. She worried her lower lip between her teeth. She needed a mastermind, someone to assist her in figuring out the puzzle.

Glancing at Sandrine, she weighed the pros and cons, but soon dismissed the idea. Sandrine was not worthy. Knowledgeable? Yes. But too brusque to count on.

"Think, girl. If the fae can break their curse and walk among us, even if they must hide from daylight, we will not survive. If you think they will honor the agreement they set with you, you are wrong. They have tricked me more than once; it is better not to hope, and I see the spark in your eyes."

Maeve grimaced. "How long have you worked for them?"

Sandrine scowled and walked faster. "It's best not to get to know each other. You'll be dead once you've outlived your usefulness."

Anxiety bloomed as she sped up, recalling how the fae had treated her as a punching bag. The crack of a whip. The snap of her nose. Did the fae even want her to succeed? They'd taken the one trait that gave her an advantage above others, her strength. Destitute and in the wild, the best plan she could think of was to take on a bounty to fund her quest for the seven shards, all the while considering a way to foil the plans of the fae.

8

MASTER OF THE FAE

THE MASTER—KING Mrithun of the fae—climbed the stairs, wide slabs of stones that wound in a spiral, taking him higher and higher, up into clear air. He enjoyed the sensation of being away from the smell of blood, the rot of prisoners, and the cries elicited from the tortures.

The court of the fae had fallen. They'd always been dark, hungry for blood and twisted, malicious acts, but now they were lost, corrupted, trapped in the dank, dark Underground. Often their actions were for sport, a way to amuse themselves during the long dark days when they longed for sunlight, starlight, moonlight, anything other than the stifled heat of the Underground. It was as close to the Underworld as they'd ever be. Their exile was payment for their sins, wickedness, and desire to rule the world. The curse had been a devastating blow. Time and time again, Mrithun had analyzed the details of the war. He'd led his armies to the height of civilization—the kingdom of Draconbane—only to be set back because he misunderstood how powerful the race of dragons were. He'd used his black magic to create a curse, and somehow, the curse reflected back on him and his people. The dragons were no longer the most powerful rulers in the world, but the fae were also banished from sunlight.

Salvation was nigh, and once the curse was broken, he would take the name of king again and rule the court with an iron grip. New laws would be applied, for he had plans for his court and plans for his queen. All those years ago, she'd beckoned, and he'd come running, besotted, but not anymore. She hadn't warned him about her sister, nor the dangers of her land. Forgiveness had been given, but just because he forgave did not mean he forgot. There was also the Prophecy of Erinyes to consider, and he intended to rise as the prophecy came true.

Ah, but the years had been long, and the remaining months were bittersweet. In truth, he missed the light of the sun on his face, the song of the bird, the cries of the night hunters and his castle hidden deep in the woods. He missed the freedom. But patience was his weakness; he had made missteps, and it was taking time to recover from them. It was a risk to collar Maeve of Carn and bend her to his will. But if all did not go well, he had contingencies, and his queen was smart, always thinking ahead. At times, he wondered if she meant to blindside him, and so he stayed alert, sharing much and yet still hiding some of his plans from her. He understood the need to play his hand and hold out in case she tried to overthrow him.

Deep in thought, he made his way to his chambers, shedding his robes as he walked. His queen preferred him without the mask he hid behind, and he knew why. Fae were known for their cruel beauty, sharp features, hard eyes full of depth, and lips that thinned and curved back to reveal fangs or a row of sharp, pointed teeth. The appearances of the fae varied; some were beautiful, while others dwelled in beast form, for their fae form was enough to make one lose their wits. The Master's own form was a cross between devastating beauty and horror, hence the mask he wore to keep from distracting others with his appearance.

He removed the mask as he glided up to the door of his chamber and entered. Shutting the heavy door behind him, he turned to take in his dwelling place. The rooms were spacious, with high ceilings, as close to earth as could be in the Underground. Torchlight lit up the interior of the room, and black and red satin drapery hung from the dark stones of the walls and ceilings. The first room was his bedroom, and beyond that were his work rooms, filled with old scrolls, weapons, and conquests of war—mostly bones and treasure. He bared his fangs at the sight of the delightful creature who lay on the bed. She rested on her side, facing away from the door, her golden wings folded on her back and her slender form covered in a silk dress, thin and as delicate as a spider's web. One flick of his claws would rip it to shreds, and he would relish the pleasures of her naked body.

She turned at his step, sitting up and dropping the scroll from her fingertips. A light came to her honey-colored eyes and dimples stood out on her cheeks. Her face was round, angelic, her skin pale, and a cascade of hair as dark as his heart flowed down onto her pale shoulders. The silk covering her showed off her heavy breasts, pointed nipples, and the curve of her belly giving way to generous hips. His angel. His queen. His dragon.

"Mrithun, is your business concluded? Did the warrior agree to search for us?" Her voice was breathy and whispery, like bells that chimed gently with wonder.

"Aye, my angel." He strode toward her, his feet sinking into the plush carpets he'd stolen from houses of wealth to provide comfort for his queen.

Business. Maeve of Carn would do his dirty work for him, although he would send his warriors out every full moon to make her path easier—or more difficult. If Maeve of Carn succeeded, he'd have more for her to do, and the golden collar was a guarantee she would obey his commands. He only wished he'd been able to control the warlord, someone he assumed she cared about. It had been a mistake he'd easily rectified, yet it was difficult to exert full control with only twelve nights of the year to watch Maeve.

Still, Maeve of Carn was a puzzle, and the Master wished he had more on her. Although he'd sent Sandrine, the scholar, to guide her for a time, he knew the old woman would not be able to sway Maeve to join the fae. Nor would Maeve be able to persuade Sandrine to help her escape. Sandrine was hardened and uncaring, and although she had some weaknesses—what was left of her family—they were of no use to the fae. She'd lost everything and had bent to his will like clay in his hands, although he allowed his queen to handle most of the dealings with her. After all, it had been his queen's idea to gather the Seven Shards of Erinyes. Once Maeve of Carn completed her quest and brought him the shards, he would use his black magic to put the pieces back together, set his bride free, and break the curse that kept the fae trapped in the Underground.

He sat down on the bed beside his queen and ran his fingers through her long, dark hair. She rolled her head back and closed her eyes. A sigh came from her lips, those rosebud lips that begged for his attentions. A strap of her gown fell down, baring a shoulder to his caresses. He pressed a kiss to her arm, then her lips . . .

Her hand come up, sliding under his cloak, seeking bare skin on skin. A throaty moan escaped from her, begging for more. Passion seized him, but he pulled back, calming his thudding heartbeat, the heart he made certain no one knew he had.

"Before the year is out, I will set you free, to return to flight. We shall walk the earth and become the gods of men."

"Promises." She smiled, arching her back.

He frowned at her disbelief in him. "Promises, nay, it is the prophecy," he scolded her.

Still, she smiled up at him.

Conniving. The word pierced his thoughts, and he picked up the scroll she had dropped. "What are you reading?"

The flirtatious smile fell from her lips and she sat up, a seriousness coming to her pale eyes. "My lack of knowledge has always been my folly, my downfall," she admitted, searching his face for understanding. "I have learned much from the scholar, which makes me believe I should continue my studies without her. If we succeed in gathering the Seven Shards of Erinyes and break all curses, we must be prepared. We are not the only ones who are cursed. I've read the Prophecy of Erinyes in full, but I don't know what other beings we will set free if we succeed."

"Ah," Mrithun said as he smiled, his fangs on full display, although they did not frighten her. She loved the horror of who he was and admired his beastly looks and abilities. "You strategize to find out what we might be up against."

"You speak truth." She reached out a finger to touch one of his fangs. "We need a blade, one that can protect us. Do you think you can make one?"

He took her hand in his, passion swelling as dark thoughts twisted through his mind. "You need not ask," he told her, and reached out a hand to brush her hair off her shoulder, baring her neck to his gaze. The marks where he'd bitten her were still there, a reminder of intoxicating pleasure.

She poked him in the chest. "I see where your mind goes. Work first, then pleasure."

A low growl came from his throat. "We make our own rules here."

"Of course; Master." She dropped her gaze, her voice going husky and breathy.

The term, Master, seemed almost derogatory coming from her lips. Baring his fangs, his growl came again, louder, without restraint. He gathered her in his arms, determined to enjoy his pleasure to the fullest before setting to work once again in the endless night of the fae Underground.

9

WARLORD'S FORTRESS

"It's quiet around here," Sandrine said as they crouched behind a rock. "Much too quiet. I don't like it."

Maeve peered over the stones, eyeing the fortress that rose before them like a lion guarding its pride. "Have you been here often?" She glanced at her companion, searching for clues to fill in the gaps of who Sandrine truly was and how she had come by her knowledge.

"Enough." Sandrine shrugged. "Lord Sebastian is retired, but his warriors are restless. I expected to see them patrolling the island, riding their horses to the outpost or, if nothing else, fishing and loading their ships for another conquest. We have seen no one since we passed Lord Murphy's fortress, and I don't like it."

Maeve chewed her lower lip, unsure how to

respond. The sun hung low in the sky, casting a red sunset across the beach.

"That's Lord Sebastian's fortress, isn't it?" Maeve's gaze flickered to Sandrine's for confirmation.

"Aye, that it is. The first shard is buried in his collection of wealth," Sandrine confirmed.

Maeve used the failing sunlight to study it. Rust-red stones had been cut into blocks and piled high, covering the coast in shadows. Gray rocks and jagged boulders, large enough to sit on, lined the uphill path, a mixture of dust and sand that curved to the fortress. The tower perched on a ridge, allowing those inside to keep watch on those who came and went. Nothing would surprise the inhabitants of the fortress, and Maeve considered her options as she examined it. Her shoulders slumped, and finally she admitted it would be best to walk up to the gates, posing as a warrior for hire.

Sandrine slung off her sack and dragged out the same thick book she'd been reading when she and Maeve met. She thumbed through it, wetting her fingers with her tongue to loosen the vellum, which stuck together. "Have a look, girl."

Girl. Some of Maeve's frustration slipped out. "My name is Maeve. Would it kill you to address me by my given name?"

Sandrine merely waved her hand, brushing away the words, and pointed.

Maeve leaned over to examine the pages. The first page displayed a drawing of the fortress, but the second was only lines, marked now and then by small words or letters.

"This is a map of the keep," Sandrine explained. "Each of the fortresses in this bay have a similar design, for the same master builder built them, one who later became an ally of the fae. He provided the blueprints for the fortresses."

Sandrine pointed to the bottom of the first page. "Here are the gates, which let you into the courtyard. There are several doors here that lead to warrior's quarters, staff quarters, the kitchens, stables, and the side armory. The main armory is inside the keep, here, close to the treasury. The main entrance leads you into the hall. The first level is usually where they eat. The second level is the lord's chambers. The third level is used for defense, in case there is an attack or siege. Both are uncommon here. The fourth level provides access to the battlements. There are two places where treasure is stored. The first, the true treasury, is underground; these trapdoors on the first floor access it. The second is on the fourth floor, so raiders have to cut through all the defenses to reach the treasure. However, treasure is heavy, and not all of the warlords or their men are willing to carry it to the fourth level. Some keep a share in the hall of lords or in their chambers. Given the peace in Biscane, the shard could be in any of these possible locations."

"By the Divine," Maeve whispered, her tone hushed

in awe. "Do you carry the knowledge of the world in that book?"

Sandrine gripped the edges of the book as though Maeve might rip it away. "I am the scholar, and this is my life's work. I will reveal what you need to know when you need to know it. Do you have questions regarding the information I have given you?"

"No." Maeve glanced at the tower again. "What you have shown me is useful; I simply need to buy myself enough time to search all four levels. I will wait until sundown, enter the castle, and pretend to be one of Lord Sebastian's warriors. If that is not possible, I will ask for an audience with him to convince him to come out of retirement for a treasure."

Sandrine lifted a hand to stop Maeve. "Girl. I do not need nor desire to hear your plans. I provide the knowledge and you complete the task. How you do it does not interest me, I only care about the result."

Maeve leaned back as though Sandrine had slapped her. The scholar's harsh words reminded her she was alone. This was not a conquest like those she'd planned with Caspian; she had no one to talk through strategy and variations with should things go wrong. She needed to make those decisions alone. Maeve bit the inside of her cheek and glanced out at the sea. They were well past the Sea of Sorrows, and the waters of the Northern Sea were clear, reflecting the rays of sunset. It was said if one sailed north, they would reach the Sweet Sea, where the waters were delicious enough to drink and the creatures that dwelled within them grew abnormally large and had the most delectable flesh. For a moment, Maeve wanted to dive in the waters and sail out there. If she ran from the fae instead of completing the task, how far would they go to come after her?

Maeve squared her shoulders. Sandrine's bitterness would not get the best of her. "I see," she murmured.

"Good." Sandrine packed away the book and slung her sack on her shoulder. She hunched behind the rock, looking like an old beggar woman. "You are on your own now. I will meet you at the outpost and make arrangements for our next journey."

Maeve raised an eyebrow. "Don't you need gold for that? Where are we going next?"

Sandrine sniffed. "I will worry about that. Focus on getting that shard, unseen. You know well enough that if we start a war on this island, escaping will become difficult."

"Aye." Maeve's fingers went to her blade. "Where shall I meet you in the outpost?"

Sandrine raised three fingers. "Wildling Inn on the southern end, close to the sea. You have three days. We need to keep pace if we are to complete this task in seven months."

Ah. So, the fae had given the scholar the same time limit.

"I will meet you then," Maeve said coldly, although she wanted to ask Sandrine about the fae. What had they promised her? Why did she work for them?

Sandrine set off down the rocky path with a scowl on her face, leaving Maeve alone to face the tower.

A sliver of moonlight lit her way as Maeve strode up the rocky path to Lord Sebastian's fortress. The eerie silence unnerved her, until even the sound of the waves crashing against the rocks on the shore made her jump. Sandrine had been right. It was too quiet. She hadn't heard a single horse neigh, nor were there any sounds of warriors practicing or talking. There weren't even any warriors on the way to the seas to fish, and everyone knew the best catches would be caught after night fell, when the fish could not see the shadows of the boats.

Salty sea wind blew against her back as she reached the end of the path and froze outside the gate. The impressive structure rose higher than her head, with heavy iron doors that would take a troop of men to pull open. The doors were likely controlled by a pulley system with chains, and often a door in the side of the wall was used instead of the gates for regular foot traffic. The larger gates were generally open during the day and shut at night, when the comings and goings were few.

Maeve's throat went dry as she stared at the open gates, wide enough for three men to walk in side by side. Was it a trap?

She held her breath and silently counted to ten as she listened.

Nothing, not even the sound of footsteps.

Drawing her sword, she slipped through the gateway, steeling herself for what might be on the other side. An empty courtyard greeted her—cobblestones, a group of wells on the far side, and doors to adjacent buildings that stood wide open, welcoming the night air into their secret hollows.

Maeve's gaze shifted, searching for archers and other warriors who should be defending the tower. The wind blew again, but the stone walls blocked out the sea air, and this time a foul scent wafted to her nostrils. She sniffed. Dung. Decay.

Something white flapped in the wind, nailed onto the main doors to the keep, which, according to Sandrine's instructions, she could use to access the four levels. Still expecting a trap, Maeve crept toward the doors. Rubble crunched under her feet, and she held her sword in front of her, fully expecting warriors to pour out of the door and take her down.

The white item moved again. When she walked up the four stone steps to the doors, she saw it was a scroll nailed into the arched doorway that framed the keep. The doors were cracked open as though someone had been fleeing and swung the doors shut behind them. Words written in ruby red blood were scrawled across the scroll. Maeve pinned the flapping end of the scroll down with her finger and read:

Twelve hours of moonlight was not enough.
Finish what we started . . .

A muffled cry escaped her lips. She pressed her hand against her mouth as bile rose in her throat. Eyes wide, she scanned the courtyard again, even though she knew it was in vain. The night of the full moon had passed. The fae had gone, but not before they spent twelve hours warring through the keep. They'd likely slaughtered everyone inside as they searched for the shard.

Anger seeped through Maeve. It was clear they had failed, but fully expected her to finish their dirty work. After all, that was why they'd captured her. The fact that they had come before her and attempted to find it for themselves ignited a fury within her. The Master had made a deal with her, but it was clear she was their last resort. They already had the knowledge of the whereabouts for the shards, collected over years, perhaps even decades. But only being able to search once a month was not enough for them, which was why they needed Maeve to find the shards. Maeve understood their reasoning, but they had made her situation more difficult.

What if someone saw the fae attack the tower? What if someone escaped and went to the nearest tower to raise the alarm, or to the outpost? If the inhabitants of Biscane had been roused, they'd soon arrive to pick over the spoils of war, and if she were caught in the crossfire, they would kill her. Unless—by a miracle of the Divine—she got out alive.

Maeve set her jaw and ripped the parchment off the door. With a cry of frustration, she slashed it in half and stomped on it. The message was clear. Gripping her sword, Maeve kicked the door open wider and ran inside.

Bodies lined the hall, some headless, others with slashes down their chests. Some still grimaced in anger, while others held their swords, death screams frozen on their dead faces. Arms, legs, even fingers were scattered across the floor, along with ripped clothing, streaks of blood, and black, bloodied weapons. Maeve averted her eyes from the death and winced as guilt buried into her flesh like a knife. Was this how she left people after killing them? After the devastation she wrought with Caspian and his mercenaries? Was this why she was being punished? Because her sympathies did not lie with the salvation of humankind and the beauty of a single life? But there was no time to consider her guilt, so she pushed those thoughts away and ran on.

The trapdoor on the first level was easy to find. A burning torch had been left and, not expecting any resistance, she sheathed her sword and took up the torch. The stairs were damp and slick, and Maeve descended tentatively, ready to use the torch as a weapon if needed.

The yellow pool of light was tiny in the immense underground cavern. She held it up, and a structure caught her eye, along with the glimmer of glowing coals. She held the torch over it and it lit up, shooting light across the walls. It was as though she'd set off a chain reaction, and the torches across the treasury lit up. Light bounced off the stone walls, revealing the cavern.

Maeve's breath caught and her face went hot. Treasure. More treasure than she'd ever seen in her life. What a find! If this had happened before the fae had captured her, she'd have taken it all, found a ship, and set sail for the north without a care in the world. But now . . . a curse left her lips. She backed away. The golden coins that covered the floor were from tipped-over trunks, and the silk gowns were ripped apart. The treasury had already been ransacked. If the shard was there, the fae would have found it.

Spinning on her sandaled heel, she took the stairs back up two at a time, careful not to slip on blood.

She dashed toward the second level, fully aware scavengers might interrupt her at any moment. She raked her mind. Where would she keep the most precious treasure of all if she were Lord Sebastian? The treasury was not safe enough; that was where he sent his warriors to hide the loot, and likely where he paid them. No. It would be sacred. Close to him. Perhaps somewhere on the second level, close to his chambers?

Maeve had heard stories about men who lost their souls to their treasure. They'd find a jewel that made their eyes gleam, their hearts beat just a bit faster, and they'd hoard it. Each day they'd take it out, stroke it, talk to it, treat it like a well-kept mistress. Was Lord

Sebastian like that? Did he hoard his treasure and look at it with stars in his eyes? If he had one of the lost shards, it was not likely he'd told others about it. Maeve imagined he might have killed anyone who'd helped him find such a powerful relic.

She paused on the stairs, unsure whether to proceed to his chambers or go to the tower on the fourth floor. In the end, the fourth floor won. If Lord Sebastian had the tendencies she thought he had, he might have a secret place in the most fortified area of the castle. If her luck held, he'd have died close to that spot, unless the fae had taken him prisoner.

She ran as though the fae were at her heels.

10

THE FIRST SHARD

THE FOURTH FLOOR was devoid of bodies. Maeve passed one on her way up, but otherwise the halls lacked the display of violence on the previous three floors. It appeared the fortress had been taken by surprise, and all they'd managed was an unorganized rush to halt the fae.

But what if there were survivors up on the fourth floor? Would she run into a fearsome warrior set on protecting the last defenses?

Her muscles throbbed with tension as she made her way through the fortress. The tower was like a maze. She passed arched windows blowing in fresh sea air, the moonlight combining with her torchlight to help her see a few feet ahead. Each time she opened a door, her heart thudded so hard she thought it would burst, but when her eyes scanned empty rooms, she left in disappointment. Was it possible to find the shard in a matter of hours? The fae had spent all night searching, though she didn't know if they had conducted a thorough search floor by floor.

Finally, she opened the door to a room that looked promising. A high arched window let in a flood of moonlight, revealing a table against a wall with a wide plush chair. Papers and scrolls ruffled in the wind, and on the other side of the wall was a full suit of armor.

A sudden knowing struck her, as though she'd been there before, and knew this was where she needed to be. Relief seeped through her. The shard had to be somewhere buried in this room.

She set the torch in a holder by the door and walked into the room, lifting each paper and unrolling each scroll before turning her attention to the table. It was solid, without any cracks or slotted openings. It revealed nothing.

With a sigh, she knelt by the chair, using her sword to rip through the plush cushion. It gave way without resistance, and white gossamer feathers fluttered out.

Maeve ripped out the feathers, tossing them on the table, but there was nothing. She squinted at the moonlit window. How many hours had she been in the fortress? It was well past midnight, she assumed, and she hoped to be away before morning. Her reputation would not survive being discovered in a tower full of death. There was still honor among thieves, especially for warriors who wanted to work for warlords, and if her name became associated with this terrible crime, she'd never work again.

She lashed out, kicking the chair over. It landed on its side, and a hollow bang rang out. There was something under the stone. Dropping to her knees, Maeve shoved the chair over and ran her fingers over the stones beneath it. Sure enough, one was loose. Using the edge of her sword, she wedged it in the crack and pulled back to pop the stone out.

Holding her breath, she reached down into the hole. Her fingers wrapped around a shape; a box. She pulled it out, fingers tingling with excitement. Was this it?

She placed the box on the table where the moonlight allowed her to see it plainly. It was a simple box, hewn out of wood with a symbol carved into it that resembled an S with a line crossed through it. Maeve narrowed her eyes. She thought she'd seen the symbol before, but couldn't be sure. She'd ask Sandrine what it meant.

Her fingers fumbled with opening the box, and she quickly realized it was locked. Biting her lip, she debated what to do. If she smashed the box, she could end up shattering the shard—if it was inside. A broken shard would cost her, but she did not have time to search for a key, which would likely be with Lord Sebastian's effects.

By the Divine! Was nothing easy?

A silver glint appeared in her peripheral vision and she jerked back—just in time, as a knife sailed past her nose. It clanged against the stone beside her and fell to the ground.

Hot blood rushed to Maeve's fingertips. Snatching up her sword, she spun to face the intruder.

A man leaned against the door in the pool of torchlight. He had a long face, high forehead, and shoulder-length silver hair tied back with a small black ribbon. His eyes were narrow, squinty, and his nose hooked and long. His overall appearance reminded Maeve of a ferret. His clothing was rich but torn in places, and bits of dark liquid had dried on it. Blood, she assumed. Then she realized he was leaning against the doorframe because his leg was wrapped in a bandage. He spoke first, his voice deep like the waves of the sea crashing against the shore during a storm. "So. You have come."

Maeve straightened, noticing he was unarmed. Why would he throw his last weapon at her? "And you are?" she asked, more for clarification than anything else.

He touched two fingers to his forehead. "Lord Sebastian. Although I suppose you already assumed. I knew this day would come."

His voice had a sweet lilt to it, compelling, like honey.

Maeve tilted her head at him, but her fingers squeezed the box. "What day?" she whispered.

"The day you came to take the shard." He shrugged.

"Not you personally, I wasn't sure who they would send, but someone."

Maeve made a small sound in her throat. He knew about the quest for the shards. That meant she had to kill him so he could not hunt her. The thought made her tremble; she did not want to kill him, but she also understood there could be no witnesses, no one who could link her back to the stolen shard and the destruction of the castle. Fear tightened in her belly. To buy herself time, she held up the box. "How did you find it?"

Lord Sebastian's gaze moved to the window, which faced north. "I sailed north and found the treasure of treasures." His tone went wistful. "I also found meaning to life and retired from my pillaging ways."

"There is no retirement for warriors," Maeve muttered bitterly.

"That's what you think," Lord Sebastian replied evenly. "Whoever sent you is relentless. Evil. I assume they promised you a reward if you complete their dirty work for them; perhaps they even have something on you, a secret, a knowledge, or they captured someone you love or admire. But you are sealing your own doom. The seven shards should never be put back together. There is a reason curses should not be broken."

Maeve scowled, her heart pounding in her throat. She had to admit, she was curious about Lord Sebastian and what knowledge he might have. But she also hated talking to her prey before she killed it. She grunted. "I'm afraid I don't understand."

He shook his silver head. "Nay, I wouldn't suppose so. Warriors like you are all the same. You fight, giving little thought to right or wrong, good or evil. Your lack of conscience is your problem. I was like you once, young and given over to battle lust. Life and longevity can teach you much, if you will listen."

"I don't have time to listen to you," Maeve snapped.

"Ah yes. Young ones. Always in a hurry." Lord Sebastian's deep voice went hard. "One day you will regret your actions, when you come face to face with judgement."

A strangled laugh left Maeve's lips. "Judgement? I already regret my actions. You presume to know much about me when we have only just met."

"You have not shown me reason to assume you are different from any other warrior." Lord Sebastian narrowed his eyes and limped farther into the room. "Are you?" he demanded.

Maeve took a shuddering breath. Why was it important? Why did she want him to know she wasn't like the others? She wasn't a mere warrior out for blood in exchange for gold coins, a full belly, and a night of endless pleasure. Guilt pinched her conscience. "I don't want to hurt you, but my master is powerful. I must keep my end of the bargain to regain my freedom."

"We all serve a master," he sounded sad as he spoke.

"Some more ruthless than others, but if you think someone as powerful as your master will grant you freedom, you lie to yourself. The only freedom he will grant you is release from this life—in the form of separating your soul from your body."

Anger ripped through Maeve as he voiced her worst fears. Her free hand tightened around her blade and she brought up her sword. "Enough!"

Lord Sebastian's shoulders slumped and his face twisted in pain as he limped forward. "Kill me if you have to. But remember my words. We all choose. Some to do right, others to do wrong. People often believe they are backed into a corner and left with no choice. But the decision to go left or right, to let live or let die, is always yours. When you think you are stuck, it is because you are only looking in one direction. Look the other way. For that is where escape lies."

Maeve pointed her sword at his belly. "You don't look as though you want to escape."

He held his hands out, palms up. "I don't. I have lived. I set the fires when I heard you reach this level. They will be here soon."

The fires? Maeve's gaze tore to the window, where the moonlight shone in the velvet blackness of night. Stars peppered the skies and, in the distance, she heard the unending crash of waves against rocks. In the darkness she thought she saw a faint glow.

If the fire was ablaze at the top of the tower, it would be a warning to the other warlords that there was trouble on the island and to be on guard against it. Whoever was closest would send a squad of warriors to investigate, and if they caught her here . . .

As Maeve turned back, Lord Sebastian pulled a blade from the suit of armor and faced her with it, swaying on his one good leg.

Maeve's voice went tight. "Tell me where the key to open the box is."

"There never was a key," Lord Sebastian said. "You must pick the lock."

Maeve's lips thinned. She'd smash the box if she had to, but she needed to be sure it was the shard. She did not know Lord Sebastian, and although his words had unsettled her, she also believed he wasn't beyond reproach. What if he was lying to her?

He advanced, and she rushed around the edge of the table, blade raised. They met in the middle of the room, blade clashing against blade.

Maeve met his gaze as they crossed swords, and she stood her ground, pushing her weight against his. A voice in the back of her mind screamed at her to make a different choice, to let him live, but she was committed now, all guilt pushed aside, pressed down under a twisted mist of fear and rage.

Lord Sebastian's face had turned to a murderous calm as he waited for the final blow. It was the look in his eyes that sent Maeve over the edge. Using only one hand, she held her stance, brought the box up, and hurled it at him. It glanced off his head, leaving a deep gash in his forehead. His eyes went wide, his grip loosened, and he stumbled, losing his balance. His arms waved wildly, but his backward momentum was too strong. As he fell, his head crashed against the suit of armor. It fell with an echoing din.

Maeve was on him in a moment. She leaped over his flailing legs, raised her sword above his heart, and brought it down hard. Her blade sank in until she heard the dull thud of the tip of her sword meeting the stone floor on the other side of his body.

He moaned and coughed. A stream of blood burst from his lips and dribbled down his neck. "You will pay," he whispered.

His head lolled to the side, his eyes rolled up in his head, and he went still.

Maeve pulled her blade free, hesitated, then cleaned it off on his tunic. Adrenaline pounded in her ears as she reached for the box. The bloom of blood on one corner made her wince. She'd been forced to kill him. Hadn't she? She had no choice. Her hands shook. Since when had she gone soft?

Pushing whispers of unease to the back of her mind, she moved back toward the table, found the knife that had been thrown at her, and used the sharp tip to pick the lock.

Her hands were sweaty and her vision kept blurring. Every now and then she glanced up at the moonlight, knowing she needed to flee the fortress before she was caught. But first, she had to know what was inside the box.

At last, the lock gave way with a click. Tossing the knife down, Maeve yanked the box open.

Pale blue light shone out. Nestled in the box amid a bed of straw lay the first shard.

11

ROGUE OUTPOST

TWO DAYS LATER, Maeve stood on a grassy knoll looking down at the outpost beside the shimmering sea. The blue waters twinkled, as though the nightmares of the bay had never happened. After discovering the shard, she'd run as fast as her feet would carry her back outside. When she'd stopped to listen near the main gate, she hadn't heard footsteps approaching, so she went to the stables. Her actions were rewarded, for there were horses. She chose a brown mare, tossed on a saddle, snatched up a saddlebag with a pouch of gold coin, and galloped across the rocky landscape into rolling hills. Following Sandrine's instructions, she stayed close to the sea. During her two-day journey, she saw other warriors, but no one raised an alarm regarding Lord Sebastian's tower, and she assumed she was safe. For now. Still, she was eager to reach the outpost and blend in. She had a full day and night before she needed to meet Sandrine. She was curious where they were heading next, but the freedom of being on her own was intoxicating.

Maeve slapped the rump of the mare. "Go on then," she said, not wanting anyone to recognize it as one of Lord Sebastian's horses.

The mare nudged her shoulder and put its head down, grazing in the long stalks of grass that grew in the hillock. Maeve shrugged. "Suit yourself."

Slinging a saddlebag on her shoulder, Maeve strode toward the outpost, also known as the Village of the Lawless.

The outpost was a walled town full of inns, trading posts geared toward warriors and mercenaries, and training grounds. Some sport could be had there, and warriors often went there to lie low or look for another warlord to work for. There was another village on the southern end of the bay, but for those who lived on the island—and needed some entertainment—the outpost was prime territory.

Maeve took her time walking toward it, though she kept an eye on the sky. The gates were open during the day, but as soon as night fell, they were closed. Wild animals hunted the bay at night, and were often drawn to the outpost by the scent of blood. After one too many wild animals had enjoyed a meal of human flesh, the walls were put up. There was also a pervasive fear of the Sea of Eels, which surrounded the Bay of Biscane on the eastern side. Many believed sea serpents claimed that portion of the sea, and the serpents were blamed for hindering ship journeys to the Draconbane Mountains.

Even without the Sea of Eels to get through, few would likely have traveled to the Draconbane Mountains, as no one wanted to disturb the dragons. That is, if there were any dragons left. The fae had supposedly slain them all over five hundred years ago, but across the Sea of Eels to the east, the Draconbane Mountains still awaited. It was said fearsome beasts had taken up residence there when the dragons disappeared. Maeve had a sinking feeling that one of the shards was hidden in those mountains. The fae had not made her task easy.

Maeve was too weary to worry about such rumors. There was a hollowness in her gut and a blanket of discomfort hovered above her shoulders. She'd slept fitfully the last two nights and knew there were black circles around her eyes. A hot bath and warm belly might help her feel better, and with the gold she'd stolen, she could secure a room and hide until her rendezvous with Sandrine.

Prayers rose like swirling winds in Maeve's thoughts, but when she opened her mouth to say them, they dried like dust on her lips. She knew it was guilt that gnawed at her. It sat in the center of her being like a dark hole, sucking away peace and all hopes of happiness, leaving her with nothing. Nothing but gloom and despair at the darkness in her soul that she seemed unable to escape.

Once again, she'd added to her personal darkness by killing someone who did not need to be killed. A choice had been laid before her and, like always, she chose the easy way out, dealing death instead of mercy. Her future lay scrawled in front of her, sealed in stone. The darkness in her soul was what the fae preyed on. If she could not conquer it, she would be their prisoner forever.

Deep down, she knew why she'd given in. Standing victorious at the end of the battle, a quest, or a heist was what she lived for. Winning brought a rush of excitement that filled her like a cup brimming over with pleasure. The delight of it thrilled her, renewed her with the rebirth of conquest. But not today.

Shoulders slumped and heart crumbling with the guilt, Maeve crept through the gates of the outpost like a thief. She tilted her head to avoid meeting the eyes of those around her. They merely glanced her way, obviously noting her as a newcomer, but one who, like them, was armed to the teeth and simply there to meet someone, hide from the law, or conduct business. Whatever it was, they'd all done it before. This was the warrior and mercenaries' land of luxurious inns, flowing ale, heavy beer, sweet, intoxicating wine, and the ability to lie back, hide, relax, and forget.

Maeve's footsteps slowed, and she surveyed the path ahead of her. A mix of stone and wooden buildings from which traders shouted out their wares and duel masters called out bids for the fight that evening rose on either side of the winding road. Whores hung out of second-story windows, their bosoms spilling over their bodices as they made eyes at the men—and women—hoping for a romp of passion ending with a pouch of gold.

The outpost was a vibrant village, alive at all hours of the day and night and always filled with sound. It echoed with rough voices, drunken laughter, screams of passion, and the clatter of horse hooves and wagons against the cobblestones The stink of flesh, dung, and raw fish assaulted her nose the strongest, but underneath was the scent of beer and the delightful smell of meat being roasted. It would take a day to walk the outpost from end to end, and it would cost almost an entire pouch of coins to sample the delights awaiting those in need of a mental escape.

Boisterous cheering jolted Maeve out of her reverie. Toward the beginning of the village was its most popular attraction, the fighting rings. Warriors often went to duel one on one, practice their fighting skills, and get a taste for blood. The rules were simple. There was a fee to enter, and after a certain number of rounds, the winner would take away a pot of gold and bragging rights. Depending on what kind of duels they took part in—first blood, first broken bone, or to the death—they would also take a trophy that could be used to help gain their next meaningful employment.

Maeve's stomach heaved at the scent of blood, and she touched her belly in surprise. She used to enjoy the duels, both watching and taking part. There was something about the eager fever of the crowds and their lust for violence and blood that used to draw her. Now, as she turned away, heading farther into the outpost, she realized duels were the warriors' way of desensitizing their minds and spirits to the ugly reality of fighting. Perhaps the fae were correct. She'd done wrong and needed to atone for her sins. Would the Divine grant her forgiveness? Give her another chance to live a life without murderous intent?

Her fingers went to the golden collar around her neck. It hummed with heat, and a white spark made her snatch her fingers away. She'd do anything to get rid of it.

"Maeve?"

It sounded as if the wind had hushed her name. But there was a familiarity to it. The open spaces of the outpost angled off into rows of buildings with alleyways and wide streets covered in a combination of dust and sand. Maeve turned slowly, then backed up toward one of the alleyways. If someone recognized her, it would be wise to be on guard. In the alley, she could keep the wall at her back to avoid being unexpectedly stabbed. There was a reason the outpost was called the Village of the Lawless. The strong survived while the weak were often mugged, beaten, and left to die—unless they had allies.

"Maeve of Carn!" the voice shouted, and then she heard footsteps.

By the Divine! Had someone seen her leave Lord

Sebastian's fortress? Ducking into the alley, Maeve pressed her body against the wall and put a hand to her sword. Sunlight still shone in the sky, but it was dim and cool inside the alley. Toward the end of the alley she saw a man stretched out, sleeping, but she decided he was too far away to be of harm. When she turned back, what she saw made her heart stop. Her fingers dropped from her hilt and her mouth trembled. She wanted to run, scream, and cry, all at once. Kneel on one knee and ask forgiveness. Her heart leaped and shattered in one instant, and she pressed her hands together to hold back the relentless wave of emotions.

It was him.

Caspian.

He walked toward her, confusion and questions dueling across his handsome face. He was a big man, half a foot taller than her, with hair the color of sunshine tied back from his face. The shadow of a beard crossed his dimpled jaw, but his face was free from scars, a wonder considering his lifetime of battle. But it was his soulful brown eyes, deep set and haunted, that had always struck Maeve.

She fell to her knees, head bowed as thirty days of pent-up emotions burst free and tears streamed down her cheeks. That familiar sensation washed over her like a jug of cool water poured over her head, refreshing her from the journey. Her fingertips tingled, and a warm glow settled in her belly. His presence made her feel as though she were wrapped in comfort, where no evil could touch her. She'd fought the feeling the first time she felt it, the connection to him, the yearning, and as she knelt in the dirt, she realized she was still fighting. All her life, especially after what had happened in Carn, she'd focused on fighting and pushing others away, always ending relationships and killing off connections after a job was done.

"Maeve." His hand touched her head, warm and comforting. "What happened? After the raid, I couldn't find you . . . I thought . . . It's been a full moon . . ."

Maeve's shoulders quaked, not with fear, but shame. It was his approval she burned for most, his admiration, even though she was headstrong and haughty when they quarreled. Their last fight, before she was taken by the fae, seemed foreign considering the predicament she found herself in now.

His fingers wrapped around her arms, and he pulled her to her feet. Using his knuckles, he gently tilted her face to his, brushing her tears away with the pads of his thumbs. "Whatever it is, you can tell me," he whispered, voice twisted with emotion.

Maeve bit her lip and shook her head. "I'm sorry," she blurted out. "I'm so very sorry."

Sliding her arms around his waist, she buried her head in his chest and held on as though he were the one thing that could save her from drowning. He smelled like the sea, a combination of salt and a fresh wind. The hardness of his armor pressed into her cheek, but beneath it there was warmth.

She inhaled, surprised at how much she'd missed him.

He returned the embrace, holding her tight, his chin resting on her head.

Maeve took one shuddering breath after the other, eyes squeezed tight as she tried to forget about the dungeon, the whip of the cruel fae, and the Master's dark desires. The shards. Should she tell him about the quest? Could she drag him down with her?

"Maeve, you're scaring me," he murmured, stroking her back. "This is not like you. You are strong, brave, and I've never seen you shed a tear, not even when that overgrown worm bit you, or when that paladin wounded you during the raid at the citadel."

Maeve nodded into his chest, although hope flittered away like petals on the wind. She wanted to stay in the warm safety of his arms, for it felt like the Master could not reach her there. Caspian had been like her, but he'd repented, changed his ways; he'd become a champion of the light, the Divine. He'd been right all along, and now she understood. Perhaps during her quest for the shards, she could speak with a priestess and ask about repentance. But how could she truly change her heart when anger sizzled in her very bones? It was built into her, into who she was. Could she rise above her past to become noble, like Caspian? A protector, a defender of righteousness?

Letting go, she met his gaze. When she tried to pull

farther away, he dropped one arm, but kept the other around her waist.

"I was taken," she offered him, unable to hide from his searching gaze, "by the fae."

His jaw clenched and his brows lowered. A thunderous expression crossed his face. "What did they do to you?" he demanded.

Maeve flushed. "It is not what you think, they did not defile me that way, but . . . there is much to tell you." Regret crept into her voice. "I am sorry we quarreled. You were right, you've always been right."

Caspian sucked in a deep breath and glanced away. "Maeve. I . . ." He shook his head. "Come. I have a room at the Bawdy Sailor. We can discuss everything there, and I daresay you're in need of a tankard or two of ale."

One of his lips curved up, a shadow of his teasing grin. "Maeve, I thought you were lost to me. The Divine has blessed our paths to meet again, and for that I am thankful."

The gloom surrounding Maeve lessened, and her shoulders relaxed. They were in the outpost, of all places, but whenever she was with Caspian, she felt like she was home. The thought surprised her. Blushing, she glanced down the path and nodded. "I'd like that. It's been long since I had a drink."

"Good." He released her and they fell in step together.

"Why are you here?" Maeve asked him. "I expected you to be on the mainland, or at least headed to the citadel or the wildlands. Why return to the Bay of Biscane?"

"I heard a rumor, and I had to be sure," Caspian said. "One of Lord Arnold's spies reported strange events taking place here. Shadows during moonlight, beasts drained of blood, and fortresses entered and searched, although it seemed nothing was taken, just destroyed. It's against the code here, and I wondered who could do such things. Especially here. Do we have an unknown enemy? And then last night, I saw that the watch fire of Lord Sebastian's tower was lit. Strange things are happening, and although it is not my responsibility, I am curious. Why target the warlords, and why now? The bay is rich with wealth, but there is enough for all."

A shiver went down Maeve's spine and her face flushed. She had answers for him, but would he like them? Would he help her figure out how to escape the fae? Lord Sebastian's words rang in her mind. Curses should not be broken. The fae should not get the shards, but how? How could she stop them?

A vision of the shard, of how the ethereal blue light had shone softly from the object, hung in her memory. It seemed so small, insignificant, just the length of her hand, and yet the potential chaos it could cause was inconceivable.

"I know why," Maeve said. "Caspian, there is much to tell you."

12

THE BAWDY SAILOR

MAEVE HUNCHED in a corner of the Bawdy Sailor, waiting while Caspian ordered from the bar. He had chosen the windowless corner wall. The inn was built into a series of connected buildings facing the street, with exits to the narrow alley that ran behind the row of buildings. It was a place where warriors could easily escape and thieves could hide in the shadows. The inside was loud, with men talking, a group of entertainers singing and carrying on, and the women from the brothel sneaking inside to try to woo men away to a night of lust and passion.

In the middle of the room was the bar, where frothy tankards of ale were brought forth and wine was poured. The barkeep sat behind it, perched on a stool, every so often hollering orders to the kitchen. A swinging door behind the bar connected to the kitchen, and a delightful fragrance filled the air, shutting out the hoppy, wheat-like smell of ale. If nothing else, the Bawdy Sailor was known for its pies: great flaky crusts stuffed with all manner of seafood, mostly thick cuts of white fish, and dripping with sweet gravy.

Maeve relaxed as she watched Caspian's broad back, his gray cloak tossed over one shoulder, arms crossed, and legs spread while he waited. That familiar stance that showed both total control and an alertness to any unexpected event that might crop up. She appreciated that about him, his keen sense of preparedness and protectiveness. Yet . . . should she tell him about the Seven Shards of Erinyes? If he were on a quest, she did not wish to add to his burden, and yet, there was no one else she could or would ask. She cursed, wondering why she'd allowed herself to have so few friends. True, the life of a warrior did not encourage friendship, but she had always held herself away, afraid of getting too close to those whom she would only fight with for a season. With Caspian, everything had been different. The way his presence had affected her made her want to stay, to gain his confidence and lean into him, no matter how short their time together might be. When he turned around, two brimming mugs in his hands, her resolve melted. She was too selfish to push him away.

He slid into the seat across from her, leaned over the table—more like a shelf, with only a foot of space between them—clinked his mug against hers, and winked. "To finding each other." He smiled, his voice filled with warmth.

Maeve wrapped her fingers around the cool mug and drank, the frothy liquid sliding down her throat before buzzing and tingling in her belly. The tightness in her muscles faded and she met Caspian's concerned gaze. There was a wary flicker in his eyes, but it disappeared as his fingers brushed against her bare arm. "Maeve, tell me what happened."

To give herself time to decide where to begin, she took another sip, enjoying the sensation the dark liquid gave her. Thirty days without proper food and drink; she had missed it.

Caspian's gaze dropped to her neck, and his eyes went dark. "Maeve. Is that what I think it is?"

Tears pricked, and she hastily blinked them away. A flush covered her neck as her fingers touched the collar. It was a mark, a sign of a slave, as insignificant as it seemed. She wished she'd worn her hair down to cover it. If Caspian noticed what it was, surely others would.

"It was that night," she spoke low, her words intended for his ears only. "After we finished fighting the slavers. I remember the moon was high, and I'd fought on, leaving the others behind. I know you'd warned me before about going off alone without someone to watch my back, but the slavers were dead and the prisoners were free. If someone sprang up on me, I thought I could take them. I was retracing my steps and leaving the prisons when I heard a low keening sound, a cry. I thought it was another prisoner, so I turned around to re-enter the building, and that's when they attacked. There were four of them, as silent as though they'd stepped from the very shadows themselves. I felt claws sink into my arm, and before I could bring my sword up the collar went around my throat. I . . . I couldn't breathe—I couldn't fight. My strength faded, and . . ."

The words tasted like dry ash in her throat. She trailed off as the memory of that night brought back a whirl of emotions. Panic, frustration, and shame shifted into something else. Anger. Fury. How dare the fae treat her like a slave, a pawn to use to fulfill their own wishes? Another part of her knew she deserved it, but she couldn't remember why. It hadn't been her first encounter with the Master, and she knew her mercenary life was somehow because of him. But she couldn't remember if she'd made a deal with him when she was young or if there was another reason. Something to do with the destruction of Carn?

She took another sip, waiting for the intoxication, the out-of-control euphoria, to ascend. "They locked me up in the Dungeon of the Damned for thirty days. That's why you could not find me. I did not leave because we argued . . . I was taken and held against my will."

He listened, nodding along, though his eyes were still dark with anger. "If I had known—"

Maeve held up a hand. "You could have done nothing. Not if you value your soul. They forced me to make a deal. Caspian." She held his gaze. "I made a deal with the Master. If I find and deliver the Seven Shards of Erinyes within seven months, he will set me free."

Caspian's breath caught, his face went white, and his hands balled into fists around his empty mug. He set his jaw and shook his head. "Maeve, I should have been honest with you sooner. You can't—"

"I can." Maeve interrupted, almost surprised by the firmness in her tone. "They sent me a scholar named Sandrine, who knows the location of all seven shards. I've already found one here in the bay, which explains the odd behavior you've heard of. The fae are one step ahead of me at all times, even though they only have those brief hours of moonlight each month."

Caspian turned, a frown on his face as he examined the room. "Where is the scholar now?"

"I am supposed to meet her at the Wildling Inn, tomorrow night. She will share our next location. Caspian, I don't have a sense of this mission, this quest. I don't know whether I should trust Sandrine. She's old and angry. I don't know whether she works for them or if she's simply a tool, like myself."

Caspian's fist slammed into the table, making the mugs jump and resettle on the wooden surface. The noise was lost in the din of the tavern. "Maeve, this quest, this task—it goes against the Divine, the laws of nature, everything. You must escape."

Maeve leaned closer. "I agree. I . . ." She paused. What would he think of her? She was damned, but she wanted, nay, needed him by her side through this. With a sigh, she related what Sandrine had told her and shared her encounter with Lord Sebastian.

He listened, fists clenched, a muscle in his jaw twitching.

She finished, barely daring to breathe as her final words left her lips. "I have it, Caspian. The first shard. But I don't know what to do. I have to continue on with Sandrine, but I need a plan, a way to turn this around on the fae. I don't know what they intend to do once freed, but we can assume they will walk this world and corrupt it with their soullessness. I know I haven't cared much for others, but now I see, I understand what it's like to have something precious snatched away. I want my freedom, I want my strength back, but at what cost?"

Caspian sighed and scrubbed at his face. "Maeve, this is a puzzle. We need more information from the scholar."

"We?" Maeve raised her eyebrows, careful to keep the joy from showing on her face. She had succeeded in tempting him.

He leaned across the table, his eyes flickering to the collar. He touched it with two fingers and then lifted his eyes to hers. They were intent. She recognized that look; the look of someone who would not be argued with. The heat of his breath brushed her lips when he spoke. "Maeve, regarding our disagreement, our quarrel, I must bring it up again. You see, I've been looking for a quest, a true quest, something beyond our . . . my . . . warring nature that wouldn't leave a blot of darkness on my soul. I want to do something beyond accumulating wealth, something purposeful, that matters beyond this life and makes a difference. I want to do something noble."

Maeve slumped in her chair. Did he have his own quest? Did it mean he wasn't going to come with her? Caspian had everything. He was a warlord with faithful warriors who respected him and followed his every command. Strife and competition among his warriors was rare. During the year Maeve had spent with them, she hadn't had to deal with the kind of cutthroat mercenaries that she'd met during her service to other warlords. But when Caspian changed his stance, he'd lost some warriors who weren't ready to follow him on his unusual path, on his mission to set things right and grow in the grace of the Divine. She was aware of the attraction between them, but Caspian had seemed determined to ruin it with his selflessness, with his desire to set the world right. However, she understood now. After all he'd seen, why shouldn't he try to make things right, even though it was impossible? And yet, despite the conflict in her heart, she forced the uneasy feelings down and listened, *really* listened, to his words.

"What I've done in the past, what *we've* done in the past, was wrong. I am done with the old life and our old ways; I've spoken with a priest of the Divine. It is a quarrelsome point between us, I am aware, but I need you to hear me, and know this. Despite our past, our history, I care deeply for you, more than you know. I would see you free again, and this collar destroyed. I would thwart the plans of the fae, not because they affect you, but they affect the world. So, I am coming with you. I doubt the fae will object to more warriors joining in your quest, and should they ask, tell them I expect payment in gold. We don't know enough, but there has to be a way to stop them and gain your freedom. We need to start with the scholar; she knows much more than we do, and perhaps there is a way."

Maeve flinched and focused on the ale as Caspian pulled back, giving her space, allowing her to think, breathe, and consider a response without overwhelming her with his presence. Desperation clawed at her—she needed a friendly face during her quest—and his words were not surprising to her. She had already sensed how much he cared, and their chemistry was palpable, but the fact that he would come with her both excited and frightened her.

Finishing her ale, she drummed her fingers on the table. "Caspian . . ." She hesitated, torn. He was coming with her because he cared, but also because it would set his mind—his soul—at ease. He would fulfill a quest, and in stopping the fae, do something noble. Something she could be part of. All the pieces fit. Stop the fae, gain freedom, stay with her best friend, and earn redemption for her soul. Was she ready?

A lad walked up just then with two steaming

seafood pies. Flakes of crust drifted onto the old wood of the table as he set the plates down in front of them. He was young and skinny with a pockmarked face, but his eyes were alight, glimmering with youthful anticipation of a bright life ahead of him. He clasped his hands in front of his chest and gave a bow. "More ale?" he asked.

Caspian flipped him a coin. "Aye, make it a double."

Maeve's anxious thoughts faded as she bit into the pie. Flavors of fish and crustacean, all baked in a thick white sauce, melted in her mouth. Food. She had not tasted such delicious food in over a month. She stopped shy of letting a groan escape her mouth. For the next few minutes, a silence stretched between them as she spooned mouthful after mouthful down her throat.

Two more rounds of ale were brought and Maeve sat back, buzzing from a slight intoxication and smiling at Caspian, who ate and drank vigorously across from her. The drink filled her mind, pushing out all other thoughts and concerns. The seven shards faded into the background until at last, when she stood to relieve herself, the world seemed to pitch and dance.

Caspian gripped her forearm to steady her.

A giggle escaped her lips. Her hand came up, flat against his chest where she felt the quick rhythm of his heartbeat. Thud. Thud. Thud. Against her hand. Blood rose to her cheeks. "Caspian. I—"

He shook his head, steering her away from the table. "Come. Let's get you cleaned up."

13

ROOM IN A TAVERN

MAEVE STEPPED from the bath and pulled on her shift. She felt clearheaded after bathing, although the buzzing sensation of ale lingered somewhere in the back of her mind. When she came around the curtain, Caspian was already in bed.

He lay on his back, one arm flung above his head, the other stretched out. Was it an invitation? Maeve felt bold. Reckless. This could end so soon, whenever the fae chose to activate her collar and drag her back down to their Underground. Trailing her wet braid over one shoulder, she sat down on the bed, her back to him.

A sigh left his lips. Encouragement? She lay back, barely daring to breathe, tucked her head onto his shoulder, pressed her chest against his side, and curled her legs next to his. His arm came down, pressing her close, protecting her. Maeve reached her arm around his hard, toned stomach, holding on, relieved to be somewhere safe. Finally. The long days and nights of her imprisonment drifted away. They'd left her raw with anger, starved for emotion, and frightened of the future. With Caspian, she could finally let that go, let the nightmares drift away, and rest. But there was still a question that left her uneasy. Six months ago, Caspian had suddenly become concerned with the darkness in his soul. Why?

"Tell me about the priest," she whispered. "What did he say about the Divine?"

Caspian lifted his blond head and eyed her. "Are you sure?"

"When I was taken, I did not know what to expect. The fae are cruel, and they put me in a hole. I starved, and I prayed, daily. Even though the fae seek to use my abilities for their own dark deeds, I felt as though my prayers were heard. Yet, I deserve nothing. I know what I've done. Tales say the only reason the fae can capture someone is if they see the darkness in their soul, and everything I've done—even some things we've done together—have created that darkness. I'm not sure if I'm ready to make it go away, but I can't keep on feeling like this, living like this, and giving darkness a hold in my life. I don't know if I am ready to act, but I can listen. Without arguing this time."

Caspian's deep brown eyes held hers, and something passed through them. Maeve dropped her gaze and tucked her head firmly against his shoulder to avoid the questions that lay there. It was easy to bare her soul with Caspian, sometimes too easy.

"Months ago, a misfortune befell me," Caspian began, his voice slow and rich. "I realized I had to change my ways or risk losing everything. I went to the Temple of the Divine in Isdrine and spent thirty days there. It was enlightening, but what I learned there isn't something that can easily be shared. I don't know how to explain it, for it's more of a sensation, a feeling, a knowing in my head and heart. You want to hear, to listen, to understand, but understanding something as powerful as guidance from the Divine isn't as simple as sharing my experience. You must seek, discover, and experience for yourself. The priests and the priestesses cannot make you whole, they cannot give light to your dark heart; you must make the choice to have faith and change. I suspect what you feel right now is guilt for the things we've done. We killed people, allowed the wrong people to come to power, and destroyed families. We were lost in our lust for wealth, for passion, and for purpose, but when you take the time to dwell on all things holy, an understanding will come over you. And that journey you will have to take alone."

Maeve lay still and a cool sensation of numbness came over her. Even with Caspian right there, she felt alone, as though the warmth of his body could not touch her. Could not pull her back from the brink and redeem her. After a moment, she realized he'd fallen silent, waiting for her response. Her thoughts muddled and converged, and her limbs went heavy. Exhaustion crept around her, pulling her eyelids shut, dragging her down to a slumber of nothingness. "I don't understand," she whispered.

"I felt the same way when the priest spoke to me. We are warriors. Give us a plan and we can follow through, but spirituality and faith are ambiguous to us. We don't understand the spiritual aspect of life because we are so focused on the physical. That's why you have to discover the revelation yourself. I can tell you what it feels like, but you will never understand until you have that connection, that meeting with the Divine."

Maeve paused. "Meet the Divine? But that is impossible. The celestials are far above us in their paradise. Why would they pay any attention to this world and races who are so far beneath their notice?"

"The Divine is not as far away as you think. You said it yourself. While you were in the dungeon, you prayed for deliverance and your prayers were heard. You have many doubts, but you also have the most important trait. Faith."

Maeve considered his words, and yet they still made little sense to her. She opened her mouth, but his words floated to her ears before hers could escape her mouth.

"Sleep, Maeve. You've been through a lot and deserve a night of rest before we face the many challenges to come."

There was a light pressure on her forehead, and then her eyelids closed and she faded away.

She floated in nothingness before sinking deeper into a dreamless sleep. Sleep rode her like the waves of the Sea of Sorrows, pushing her back up to the shallows where dreams of the child and the screaming mother plagued her mind. She woke, sweating, heart racing, and alone.

Maeve was lying on her back, taking deep breaths to calm her panic, when she noticed a blue glimmer out of the corner of her eye. Heart in her throat, she tilted her head back and saw him standing by the arched window.

Caspian had lit a candle, which gave off a small pool of light, but it was the item in his hand that gave Maeve pause. It was the shard. *Her* shard. The hairs on her neck stood up, and her body went rigid. What was he doing with it? And why would he go through her things?

He turned it in his hands, examining it from every angle before lightly placing it back in the box. It closed under his fingers; the lock made a light clicking noise. Standing, he dropped it with her armor and padded back toward the bed. His face was pale in the wan light and he scratched his chin. "Maeve?" he asked.

Maeve bolted upright, glaring, a thousand questions rising on her tongue. "What were you doing with it?" she demanded.

His eyes narrowed. "Does anyone else know about this quest? Is there anyone else who might search for the shards?"

Maeve swallowed down her fleeting anger. "Just the fae. Why?"

Caspian sat down on the edge of the bed, his hand resting near her thigh. "The fae gave you seven months to complete the task, an impossible task, of finding these lost celestial relics. They were careful and sent you a guide, but what if you're not the only one they sent out? The fae can appear once a month during the full moon, but they can use their portals to go anywhere they desire. It stands to reason this is not the first time they have sent someone after the shards, and it is not impossible for one or two to appear from time to time. Maeve, it . . ."

He paused and looked away, his jaw tightening as if he were considering something. Then his shoulders slumped and he turned back to her. "One of the shards turned up in the citadel in the king's treasury. I'm not sure if it is still there, but if the fae knew about it, they could easily find it and take it during one of their full moon rampages. Once they get all seven shards, you will be of no use to them, and we don't know what they will do. Time is working against us. You assumed they had no shards, but I believe they might have one or two, perhaps even a few, and you were sent on this quest to get the last ones for them. Which means time is working against us. We may only have three or four months to come up with a way to circumvent their plans."

Maeve rested her hands on her thighs, her foot tapping against the bedding and her fingers drumming. "You could be right, but why tell me this? And why now? Just because you saw a shard one time doesn't mean they have them all."

"I can taste it in the air. Something is off, wrong. Warriors have disappeared before, but the last three disappearances I can think of happened during the full moon. There is a restlessness in the air, a shift, and you know I always make a plan in case things go awry. I could be wrong, but my gut tells me I am right."

Maeve bit her lip and stared at the candle flickering and sputtering against the night wind. She squared her shoulders. "There is only one course of action. We need to find out what the scholar knows."

14

OUTPOST

MAEVE'S WARINESS of Caspian fell away the next day. The idea of him sifting through her things and picking the lock of the box that held the shard had sent pinpricks of doubt through her. Yet that morning, Caspian purchased a hearty breakfast for them and offered to follow her lead, and also apologized for upsetting her the previous night with his sudden idea. Because of their history, Maeve decided to push it aside. Having the big, bulky warrior at her side was a balm, leaving her with the sensation that they were invincible. Yet, time and again, her fingers went to the golden collar around her neck, each touch a reminder that her life was not hers anymore.

Striding through the outpost with Caspian was like old times. Almost. His presence was big, strong, and between the two of them they could outfight and outstrategize anyone and anything they came into contact with. Between breaths, Maeve whispered thanks to the Divine for guiding their paths together.

After breakfast, Caspian sent a raven to his warriors with word of his whereabouts and latest quest. He noted to Maeve that, as they found more information, there might come a time when they needed his warriors to rally. Maeve outwardly agreed with him, but inwardly decided it would be too risky. It would be hard to convince Sandrine that she needed hired warriors to help find the six remaining shards—if there even were six shards left to find.

The outpost was crowded, and despite the proximity of the town to the sea, the sun beat down with too much warmth. Maeve wiped sweat from her forehead and toyed with the idea of removing her crown, but brushed away the thought and strode on, ignoring the heat.

Caspian set a quick pace, weaving through the alleys and broad streets as though he knew the outpost well. They'd never come to the Village of the Lawless together, but Maeve wondered if it was a town he'd frequented in his past. A past of violence, bloodshed, and victory. A past he'd left behind. His words of last night nagged at her. She'd have to find out for herself? What did that mean? How could she possibly discover what he had?

They left the buildings behind and continued onto a dirt road that led to the sea. Hills rose on either side, creating valleys that pointed down to the sandy beach and the sparkling waves of the deep sapphire sea below them.

Maeve lifted her face to the wind and inhaled, tasting freedom that teased at her, just out of reach. Maeve lightly ran her fingers over the collar, wondering if the fae could see and track her. Then a thought jolted through her like a bolt of lightning, so sudden and shocking she gave a sharp cry. If she could destroy the collar, she'd be free from the fae.

Caspian spun to face her, one hand out to steady her while the other fell to his hilt. "What is it?" His concerned eyes sought hers.

"It's no danger," she assured him. "I just had a thought. All this time we've been considering how to thwart the plans of the fae. I know we need to stop them from getting the shards, but you came to help me too. I just need this collar removed, and they won't be able to force me to help them."

Caspian's eyes fell to the collar. "The collar was likely created by dark magic. It will be difficult to release you from it without causing physical harm."

Maeve's face warmed under his gaze. Why did he dash her hopes so quickly? Didn't he want her to be free? "I am no stranger to physical harm, and I'll do whatever it takes to regain my freedom."

Caspian ran a hand along his jaw and glanced at the sea. "I've come across some situations now and again where someone was bound with dark magic. If we try to break you free of the collar, it will probably kill you.

And Maeve, I'd rather not gamble with your life. If we find a way, we will take it, but I would not have you mangled and disfigured because we tried to use something we do not fully understand."

Maeve scowled. "It was just an idea," she said through gritted teeth.

"A good idea." Caspian touched her shoulder lightly. "But a risk we will only take if we have to."

Anger flared within, but Maeve pushed it away. Her temper was strong, and at times she felt the fire within, all-consuming, driving her to react, strike out, use violence to gain what she wanted. But she knew there was a balance, and with the collar diminishing her strength, she had to be patient.

"Maeve?" Caspian's light touch at her elbow brought her back to the present. "This is it. How do you want to do this?"

Squaring her shoulders, Maeve stared up at the inn. It slumped on the edge of a hill, a weather-beaten two-story building that had seen better days. The entire building looked as though it would tumble down the hill, scattering shingles and tile into the sea and sand-swept meadow. The once white walls were gray, their edges softened by wind, rain, mud, and sand. Persistent wildflowers cropped up around the edges of the inn, adding color to the surrounding meadow.

Maeve frowned. Why had Sandrine chosen the most run-down place on the bay to meet? She sighed. "Let me do all the talking."

Caspian slowed. "I will follow your lead."

An odd phrase coming from his lips. Usually it was Caspian who did the leading and Maeve who backed up his plans, improvising as needed.

The sea wind ruffled the wildflowers and a slight hissing sound came to Maeve's ears. She stopped in her tracks, tilted her head, and cast an anxious glance at the sea. That sound. She'd heard it before, hadn't she?

"What is it?" Caspian turned toward the sea, scanning it before turning his gaze back on Maeve.

"I thought—" She shrugged away the thought. "It was nothing."

But it wasn't. She heard it again. A slight shifting in the waves, a rustle, a cry. Something was there and yet not there. A ripple went down her spine, and the door to the inn flew open.

A group of sailors poured out, their faces red and ruddy as they stumbled down the hill, making for the docks that lay just below where a group of boats were laid out on the sand. The men looked grubby, their skin was tanned and leathery, and their faces were hard. Maeve saw the whites of their eyes as they passed, a silent march down to the shore.

Caspian gave a low whistle after they had passed. "They dare to fish in those waters . . ." He shook his head.

Maeve glanced toward the shore. "What's wrong with the water?"

Caspian's brow wrinkled. "You don't know?"

The light wind ruffled his dark hair and a few strands came loose from his topknot. "The scholar will be able to explain the full history, for I am not sure what happened. Across the sea are the Draconbane Mountains—"

"I know," Maeve interrupted. From glancing at maps, she'd seen the layout of the country, the islands to the southwest, the king's citadel on the western coast butting up against the King's Sea. To the south and east of the citadel were obscure and unusual cities, towns, and kingdoms—however small the kingdoms ended up being. The Bay of Biscane lay north of the citadel, and across from the Bay of Biscane to the east were the Draconbane Mountains. After the fae defeated the dragons, no one went to the mountains, as some still believed a few of the dragons had escaped the fae and dwelled in the heights of Draconbane. In addition, rumors had it that the soil in the mountain range was putrid—ruined from fire—the mountains were impossible to scale, the storms were unceasing, and dark creatures dwelled there, morphed and twisted by their environment. The unconfirmed tales spread quickly, and the fear was enough to keep most away. Those who had taken on wagers to explore the unknown territory had never reappeared, and it was assumed they had found demons in Draconbane and given their souls to the reaper.

Caspian frowned at the interruption, or perhaps it was the sea. His gaze returned to the shining waters and

Maeve shivered as she waited for him to continue. "It's the eels," he admitted. "They fill the sea, and while hunting them is a sport, many have fallen to their deaths when the giant eels appear."

Maeve raised an eyebrow and poked his shoulder. "Caspian? It is not like you to be frightened of anything, especially a sea creature such as an eel."

Caspian brushed loose strands of blond hair back from his face. "It is not fear. I've seen them before. Leviathans that come out of the deep, bigger than a ship, their bodies thick and impossible to pierce, not with spear or sword. Nay, it's not fear that warns me, but an appreciation of life."

Maeve's gut twisted, and she glanced from the sea to Caspian. A sinking feeling nagged at her. She tried to push the thought away, but it remained. What if her next quest was to go into the west? To cross the Sea of Eels and go into the depths of the Draconbane Mountains to find the second shard? It would be like the fae to send her into a wild land, the untried unknown to find something they could only search for twelve times a year. Would she be able to find it? Or would she become another useless slave, falling to her death while the fae captured another soul with darkness in their heart and forced that individual to do their dirty work?

Again, her hand went to her collar. If it was removed, she would be free, and then, like Caspian, she could focus on blocking the fae from achieving their goal of putting together all seven shards. She glanced at him again, with his thick arms, his set jaw, the angular curve of his chiseled face. His presence was a beacon of solace, and now that he was with her, a yearning rose, so strong at times she could not ignore it. Her throat went thick, and she blinked hard. A wave of exhaustion cascaded around her, and she whispered, "Caspian, what if . . . ?"

His eyes met hers, emotion hidden behind them. His face went still as realization dawned. "Maeve. I did not mean . . ."

"I don't know where they will send me next," she muttered, her words coming out harder than she intended. "You are free to go if you wish it. I asked for your help because it will be impossible to do alone, and better with your company, but if you are too frightened of the possibilities—"

"Maeve!" Caspian raised his voice, cutting her off. He gripped her arm before she could dash up the path toward the inn and gently pulled her back to face him. "Maeve, I did not think. There are many dangers here, but I will not let you face them alone. If we go, we go together, even if it is into darkness."

Maeve stared, at a loss for words. He would do this for her? Selfishness fled. "Caspian, I only thought of myself when I asked you to join. You don't have to be caught up in this nightmare with me."

He opened his mouth, breath hissing between his teeth. "Maeve. Don't say such things. If it is a nightmare, we will handle it together, as we have done the past year. I lost you once, and I will not lose you again."

Maeve studied his stoic expression, trying to find what was hidden beneath it all. She suspected—aside from their ability to work well together—there was something else, but she dared not name it. She opened her mouth to respond, but he smiled, shook his head, and continued toward the inn.

15

WILDLING INN

THE DINING HALL of the Wildling Inn looked just as bad as the outside, neglected and uncared for. Sand covered the floor and dirt piled up in the corner. Cobwebs hung from the ceiling and windows stood open, letting in a mix of fresh air while expelling the strange odor that clung to the room. The inn was aptly named. The characters that crossed the threshold were slipshod, bedraggled, and unkempt, with beady eyes and hands ready to fly to their knives at the slightest offense.

Maeve led the way into the hall, eyes scanning the occupants and landing on Sandrine. She sat alone at a round table, spooning what looked like watery gruel into her mouth. Her dark hair was pulled back into a tight bun. She sat on the edge of her seat, one leg jiggling up and down as though she were impatient, or nervous.

Crossing her arms, Maeve marched up to the table and waited, towering above Sandrine, the shadow of Caspian behind her.

Sandrine's eyes shot up, and the barest hint of surprise registered on her face, quickly covered by a scowl. Peering past Maeve, she pointed an accusing finger. "Who is he?"

Maeve lifted her chin, eyes narrowed. "I had to hire some help. Due to the nature of our quest, it's not enough for me to go in alone, without help. I need extra muscle to ensure the safety of our items. I have worked with him before and he will be content to be paid in gold."

The spoon in Sandrine's hand clattered on the table, and she shoved the bowl of gruel away. Standing, she yanked up her pack and glared at Maeve. All pretense of friendliness, if it had ever been there, was gone. "Maeve. A private word." She pointed farther into the inn, toward a staircase hidden in shadows. Then her eyes locked on Caspian's face, and she sniffed. "Hired muscle indeed. Wait for a moment like a good watchdog while we discuss."

Maeve flinched at the term: watchdog. How could Caspian stand there and take it? But he played his part well, and not a word left his lips. He sat down at the table, pretending to be dumb, while Maeve followed Sandrine toward the shadows. She glanced back at Caspian, mouthing the word "sorry," but if he saw his expression did not change.

The rafters above squeaked, and the air smelled musty and moldy. Maeve wrinkled her nose, reminding herself that nothing was worse than the dungeon. Sandrine led her to a corner next to the stairway, which curved upward into gray light.

"Are you daft?" Sandrine scoffed. "What does that man mean to you? Who is he? Because whoever he is, you are giving him a death sentence."

Maeve leaned away from Sandrine's bad breath and the rehearsed words came tumbling out, "I told you earlier, I hired him to help. He's a warrior I've worked with before. He's loyal and does well with a blade, he can follow directions, and as long as he's paid in gold, he will not interfere with the quest nor try to take the shards for himself."

Maeve's thoughts rang as the lies slipped from her lips. They were harder to say than she'd expected, and for a moment her heart quailed. This was dangerous. Should she tell Caspian to run? If he were harmed or even slain because of this quest . . . she shivered and rubbed her arms, suddenly uncomfortable. The situation was terrible, but what else could she do? If she sent him away, he'd likely follow her. For him, there was more at stake than her freedom—he also felt a responsibility, a duty to the world and a calling from the Divine.

Miserable, Maeve looked away from Sandrine's penetrating gaze.

The scholar clearly did not trust her tale. She humphed and shifted from foot to foot. "You think this is a game, don't you? You've never interacted with the fae. You don't know what they are like, what they will take from you."

A flood of memories rushed to Maeve's mind. Her childhood. A kingdom by the sea. The loving voice of her mother and father, and then those bright tones that turned commanding. A sea of darkness overwhelming Carn, and then the earthquake, shaking the buildings down to their foundations, and then the invasion. An army had come with the quake. She had flashes of soldiers striking down everything in their way, burning, pillaging, destroying. She recalled running, fleeing among screams and shouts and the anger that spurred violence. And then came the memory she repressed most often, the one that made her shiver and if she thought too hard, gave her nightmares. She pressed her lips together, avoiding Sandrine's eyes, almost bodily turning away. She knew the fae, what they were capable of, what the Master was capable of. It was not her first encounter with him. That's how he knew how to collar and control her.

Their history went back further than she cared to remember. Emotions from her first encounter with the fae washed over her; the beauty and mystery of it, then the terror, threats, and empty promises. Finally, she had been left alone, freed to live as she wished. Warrior for hire became her stance, to focus on violence and to forget what it was like to be controlled.

She hadn't had faith then, for the Divine had not

seen fit to intervene with her downfall, but now she realized she'd never asked for help. She'd assumed the Divine would not want to help someone like her. The Divine was not like her, and the ways of the Divine were not ways she could understand. She'd clung to her preconceived expectations and she had been wrong. The Divine did not think the way she thought. She had to adjust her mindset, but it was difficult.

"Ah." Sandrine's single syllable startled her, and she turned back to face the scholar. "He is someone you care about." Sandrine dusted off her palms. "You are planning something, aren't you? Something to surprise the fae and get back at them for what they did to you. Don't say I didn't warn you, but I won't interfere if you plan on stopping them, as long as it does not break our quest."

Maeve clenched and unclenched a fist, the familiar fire stirring in her belly. She needed a fight to sate her anger and frustration. She wished the inn would be taken over, or that a bar fight would break out, anything to keep her temper in check. A muscle in her chin jerked and her gaze went slack. She focused again on the scholar. "Where is our next destination?"

She almost held her breath waiting for the answer, knowing what it would be.

Sandrine smirked, as if she enjoyed delivering bad news. "I've prepared for our voyage across the sea to the Draconbane Mountains. We are going to the lair of the last dragon, and there you will find the second shard."

Maeve stilled her breath as her worst fears were realized. Not there. She backed away, shaking her head. "Do the fae want us to succeed, or do they want us to die before we have begun?"

Sandrine tutted. "I do not pretend to know their ways. Gather your warrior, lover, whoever he is. You can drop the pretense with me. He is solely your responsibility, but next moon, the fae will surely take him from you."

Maeve scowled, but Sandrine had already turned around, heading toward the exit. "Wait! What preparations? Where are you going?"

She'd assumed they would stay the night at the Wildling Inn, but from Sandrine's gait she'd assumed wrong.

Darting out of the shadows, Maeve returned to the table where Caspian sat.

He half rose. "What happened?"

Maeve glanced to Sandrine's retreating form and bit back her confession. If Caspian knew the secrets she kept, of her prior engagement with the fae, with the Master, he'd leave, thinking the worst of her. After Draconbane she'd explain, tell him what she remembered from her past, although all the pieces did not fit together. There were still gaps in her memory, things she could not recall. Why hadn't she returned to Carn? Why hadn't she tried to make sense of her past? She knew why—she'd been too young....painful—but she felt now as if her past might hold the answers they sought.

"It is as I thought." She beckoned for him to join her, and they glided from the inn. "Sandrine has arranged everything, and we are going to the Draconbane Mountains. She also warned me of something." This part Caspian had to hear, to understand, even though he would not relent. He was a hardened warrior, smart, and would not be swayed away from any battle. "The fae may come for you during the next full moon."

"If they do, it will be no surprise," he reassured her.

They left the inn, almost bumping into Sandrine, who stood just outside, hands on her hips, glaring down at the sea.

"You must be our guide," Caspian addressed her in light tones. "I am Caspian, a warrior—"

Sandrine sniffed and waved a hand, brushing his words away. "Don't pretend you don't know what this is about. I warn you, if you attempt to steal any shards, I personally will have your head, and I won't use my healing abilities to restore it to your body."

Caspian's initial surprise gave way to a rueful grin. He nudged Maeve. "She has wit. I like her already."

Sandrine rolled her eyes. "We may run out of provisions long before we reach the mountains, but there is no time for delays."

Maeve glanced toward the waves as she followed Sandrine. "How will we cross? Surely you know about the eels?"

Sandrine glowered. "Less talk, girl. I've said it before

and I'll say it again. I will tell you *what* you need to know *when* you need to know it, and not a moment before. Useless chattering will change nothing. You forget, I am much older, and I have been in the service of the fae a long time. I know what power knowledge has, and I do not intend to share what I know with the likes of you."

"Not even to take down the fae?" Maeve blurted out.

Sandrine snorted. "If I thought that was likely, I would share everything I have."

Caspian touched Maeve's shoulder, his eyes warning her against saying anything else.

Sandrine led the silent party downhill, rounding the boulders toward the sandy shoreline. The boats from earlier had been removed, and in the distance, Maeve saw dots on the horizon, brave sailors fishing for eels, which would sell at a high price in the market. As life-threatening as it was, Maeve noted it was not much different from her life as a warrior for hire. Everyone had their vices and different things they were good at. Why did she judge how they preferred to spend their time or make their coin?

They continued down the shore as the sun set behind them, casting rays of glory across the waters, a sacred incantation of honor between sky and sea, like lovers joining to kiss each other. Such magnificence was lost on Maeve, however, and her heart thudded harder as they rounded the bend. An odd-shaped boat bobbed on the waters in front of them. Maeve opened her mouth, but Sandrine quickened her pace, heading straight for it.

16

SEA OF EELS

MAEVE WATCHED the sea as she followed Sandrine and Caspian toward the strange ship. The water was quiet, still, with no hints of shadows or devious souls hidden under the surface. The mirrorlike waters reflected the aging sunlight, a hint of promise, a whisper of hope. Hope of what? Maeve could not say. Out of the corner of an eye, she glanced at Sandrine, who had not slowed down as she made long strides toward the ship bobbing on the surface. If it could be called a ship. It was long, narrow, and appeared more like a floating log than anything else.

"Why is the ship shaped like that?" Maeve asked, more curious than frightened by it.

Contrary to her usual attitude, Sandrine did not sniff or offer a snide remark. She instead answered in a brusque and straightforward manner. "There are few warriors who are willing to cross this sea, and those who do demand a hefty fee. The brothers—Ingram and Imer—offered us passage across the sea in their closed ship. They claim it is impervious to any damage, but we shall see. If our luck holds, we will cross without issue. If it doesn't . . ." She crossed herself. "The eels take us. They are less dangerous than where we are going."

Maeve decided to dig for more information, using stupidity as an excuse to ask more questions. "Less dangerous? I thought we were going to the Draconbane Mountains? All the dragons are long dead, aren't they?"

"You assume too much. If you would know the truth, you must find out for yourself," Sandrine scolded.

"The brothers . . ." Caspian murmured.

Maeve noted his lowered eyebrows and hung back, falling in step beside him. "What is it?"

His hand dropped to his sword hilt. "I've had dealings with them before that went awry. Be on guard."

Maeve dropped her tone. "What dealings?"

Caspian's lips tightened, and his dark eyes narrowed. "Let's just say we did not leave on good terms."

Maeve's fingers tapped her sword hilt as a thrill rippled through her like a bolt of lightning during a storm. "If they try anything . . ."

"Ah." Caspian touched her arm, brushing her fingers away from her steel. "Remember, we need them to cross the sea, so we will stay on opposite sides of that boat . . . contraption . . . thing. No fights."

Maeve glared at him. "You are growing soft, aren't you? No fights? If they start something you have a right to defend yourself."

The corner of Caspian's mouth tugged back into a slight grin. "Oh, Maeve," he sighed. "You've always been a fiery one. But no, we will start nothing now."

Sandrine's dry voice cut through their conversation. "Are you two done making plans yet? Moonlight won't wait, and neither will the brothers. Unless you'd like to pay their fee to move your feet faster?"

They walked up to the object that bobbed in the water. The outside had been sealed and painted with tar to keep it afloat, while there were two small round windows near the side facing the sea. Realization dawned on Maeve as she gazed at it. The ship had been made to look like a sea eel.

Sandrine led them around to the side where a rectangular opening had been cut, creating what looked like a narrow plank for them to walk on. Standing in the odd doorway was a rugged man, tall and slim with dark eyes, a mustache, a broad hat on his head, and sagging boots on his feet. He was dressed in black with accents of red embroidered across his tunic. One of his eyes was covered with an eye patch.

Maeve's fingers went again to her sword hilt. No wonder Caspian had spoken grimly of the brothers. They were pirates.

The man's gaze went from Sandrine to Maeve and Caspian. His jaw tightened. "Warlords? You must pay double for them. And no steel onboard."

Rage rose like vomit in Maeve's throat, but Sandrine raised a hand, halting any impulsive move on Maeve's part and thwarting the pirate's demands. Planting her hands on her hips, she stepped up to the gangway. "Ingram, since it is your vessel, we shall surrender our weapons until we arrive. And there will be no more coin. A deal is a deal."

The pirate scowled.

Maeve glanced at Caspian, but his gaze was locked on the pirate and his fists were clenched. He was the one spoiling for a fight.

"A deal, aye," grumbled the pirate. "We take you into certain death and you increase the risk by bringing them aboard."

"You'll have their weapons," Sandrine returned. "What harm could they be to you?"

It was both a warning and an accusation. If the pirate brothers weren't strong enough to take on two weaponless warriors, what kind of pirates were they? The pirate said nothing else, and merely beckoned them inside as he stepped back into the shadows.

Maeve followed Sandrine up the gangway, surprised at Sandrine's spunk. The weaponless scholar knew how to stand up for herself, and again Maeve wondered about her. Whose side was she really on?

The pirate kicked open an empty chest as they entered the gloomy ship. It tilted under their weight as though it would suddenly roll on its side if they shifted too much. The air was stale, dry, and even the slight breeze from the ocean could not refresh it. The pirate crossed his arms and grunted at the chest. Maeve paused before unstrapping her sword and dropping it in, steel clanging loudly against the wooden chest. Caspian followed her lead, adding his knives.

Sandrine stood to the side, watching the proceedings out of bored eyes, yet one of her feet tapped. With impatience, fear, or something else?

A rustling sound came from the forefront of the ship and then a rough voice called out, "Are they here?" Another man appeared. He looked similar to the former, but smaller and leaner, also dressed in black with crimson highlights. Wavy dark hair was pulled back from his high forehead, and there was a mischievous curve to his wide lips. Instead of a mustache, he had long sideburns and the beginnings of a beard on his chin, and where his brother looked rough and rugged, he had an air of elegance, as though he would be just as comfortable in the court of a king. He grinned when he saw them. A grin full of mischief and misdeeds.

Maeve met his eyes briefly. They were the color of the sea during a storm, dark, misty, and full of secrets.

"I'm Imer," he offered after a beat. "Lord Caspian. No one said you'd be joining us." He gave a mock bow.

"Imer," the brother—who had to be Ingram—growled, his tone thick with disapproval.

"Listen, I'm part of this voyage now," Caspian said, his voice low and hard, his intent unmistakable. "I will have no quarrel with you as long as we are on this vessel."

Imer raised his brow, and a quick glance passed between him and Sandrine. It was a familiar look, as though they knew each other and could read each other's minds.

Maeve's back stiffened.

Imer lifted his broad head and ran his fingers through his waves of thick black hair. "You didn't tell them, did you?" he addressed his question to Sandrine.

Sandrine frowned. "I will share more information when I am good and ready. Now point me in the direction of the quarters, unless you'd like the eels to wash in here along with the sea water."

Maeve wanted to step in front of Sandrine and demand answers, but Caspian slowly shook his head, and Maeve realized that time would come. Currently, however, they needed Sandrine on their side. They needed the book and to know what she knew. Arguing in front of the pirate brothers would not go over well.

"I'll show you the way," Imer offered with another flirtatious grin. "But I warn ye, if any of you think of getting seasick aboard *Lucky Jane,* you'll be thinking again and cleaning up every last drop."

Ingram shut the gangway with a bang and began

hauling on a rope. He leaned back, clearly straining, although his brother did not offer any help. Little by little, the trapdoor began to close, shutting out the light.

For a moment, Maeve was back in the dungeon, stuck in the suffocating darkness, surrounded by the screams from the unearthly creatures . . . and the waiting. The fae knew the waiting was the worst part. The gold collar on her neck burned, and then the reminder was gone.

Caspian's hand landed on her shoulder as they followed Imer and Sandrine into the narrow hall. "We must be careful," he whispered.

Maeve nodded. They would speak later, but for now, she didn't like the odds.

"What is this vessel? Is it a ship?" Maeve called out to Imer.

The boat moved underneath their feet, rocking back and forth like a mother lulling a cranky baby to sleep. The sense of staleness grew deeper as they walked. A delicate balance of mistrust and treachery surrounded them like an invisible spider's web.

"I'd have to kill you if I told you," Imer said as he chuckled, his laugh echoing off the rounded walls. "My brother and I like adventure, and no one has conquered the Sea of Eels save us. We built *Lucky Jane* with our own two hands, and she is a pleasure to sail. The eels do enjoy playing with her, but they haven't broken her yet!"

Imer's excitement carried like the crackle of lightning.

He was an adventurer. A daredevil.

"Interesting. And how many trips across this sea have you taken?" Maeve asked.

"Ah, distrusted by a warrior." Imer snorted. "I could only expect as much. Just wait and see my lady, wait and see." He wagged his head sadly and patted the wall, as though consoling the ship.

Maeve scowled, and then to her relief saw lights. A low glimmer came from the wall in the form of . . . streaks of silver? Her eyes went wide. How was it possible?

"Mind the walls," Imer called, as though he'd heard her thoughts. "We used jelly from stinging fish to create eternal light, but it still stings when touched."

"Will there be vipers at the end?" Caspian asked coolly.

Imer chuckled, but this time a dangerous note sounded at the end. "As guests on this ship, I'd appreciate a little more enthusiasm and less discord."

"They'll be quiet now and leave you to your work," Sandrine snapped, turning to glare first at Maeve and then at Caspian.

Maeve sighed as they filtered into a round room. The ceiling was low, forcing them to hunch over, but otherwise the room was spacious and would allow them to lie down with ease. There were ropes attached to the rear wall, bolted down by a large hook.

"These are your chambers for the length of the journey," Imer said as he grinned, standing on the outside while they examined the room. "I'll let you know when we arrive."

In one swift motion, he yanked on a chain and an iron grating came down, locking them in the chamber.

17

LUCKY JANE

"No!" Maeve shrieked, banging her fists against the grating. For a moment she couldn't breathe. Panic rose and her vision swam. The cold, the dark, and the dank smells came rushing back. "Why are you locking us up?"

"Sit down," Sandrine hissed.

"Maeve?" Caspian's hand rested on her shoulder, the familiarity just enough to remind her that she wasn't back in the dungeon.

Imer walked backward with his hands raised, a mocking grin on his handsome face. "You'll thank me later!"

And then he was gone, disappearing through the glowing jelly back into the shadows of the bobbing boat.

Rage surged through Maeve and she slammed her fist against the iron bars, even though it was useless.

The pirates weren't coming back. At least, not until they landed on the far shore.

"You knew about this?" Maeve spat the words at Sandrine. "That the brothers would lock us in here?"

Sandrine shrugged as she backed into a corner, sitting down near the coils of rope. "It was the deal. We are going across the sea the safest way possible—aside from flying."

Maeve huffed but allowed Caspian to pull her away from the grate. Every time she took steps to secure her freedom, she ended up back where she started, and this hole made her shudder. Maeve crossed her arms, taking in their quarters.

The room smelled of old shoes and stale water. Gray and green shapes grew out of the curved walls of their prison, lacing themselves between slats of wood and iron, desperate to belong somewhere.

The floor shuddered and then pitched forward with a wild swing. Maeve was thrown against the back wall. She smacked into it with a grunt, Caspian right beside her, groaning from the unexpected violence.

Sandrine was securely tied to one side of the cramped quarters, and she glanced at them, emotionless. "Use the rope to tie up. It's not going to be a pleasant journey."

"You could have told us that sooner," Maeve complained, rubbing the back of her head. "What is going on? Are you ready to tell us?"

Sandrine sniffed. "Are you ready to claim he's not simply a hired hand?" she pointed at Caspian.

"What's it to you?" Maeve demanded, holding up a hand to ensure Caspian stayed silent.

"You don't know how dangerous this is," Sandrine said. Her gaze shifted to the iron grating, and she paused.

Maeve knotted the rope about her waist and waited. Was Sandrine about to confess? But instead of going on, Sandrine pressed her lips together, as though she'd changed her mind, and closed her eyes.

Caspian sat down beside her, his presence a welcome distraction from the gloom and stink of the hold. She glanced at him and he met her eye, nodding his understanding. Regardless of what happened, they were in this together. Again, conflicting feelings rose. Should she have dragged Caspian into this? Was it too dangerous? Would the fae threaten him? Take him?

The ship shifted again and then rolled. Maeve's hands came out to brace herself, grabbing the wall on one side and Caspian's bicep on the other. She closed her eyes as a sensation of dizziness came over her. The ship tilted again, and distantly she heard the ringing of water washing over and around them. They were pushed violently to one side, then violently to the other.

Maeve bent over, no longer trying to brace herself, and wrapped her arms around her middle in an attempt to keep her last meal inside. Were the pirate brothers insane? Maeve's senses went dull as the pitching of the ship continued, knocking them from side to side. Vaguely, she heard voices, and then her eyes closed, casting her back into the same vision she'd experienced while crossing the Sea of Sorrows.

Two people held her arms back. Tight. They were hurting her, were close to ripping her arms out of their sockets. But the pounding in her chest would not let her forget her internal pain. She fought, relentlessly kicking, biting, and scratching. Reaching the child was a matter of life and death. Fury engulfed her and burned like a raging fire as the strangers dragged the screaming child farther and farther away. And then she was free. Picking up a stick, she turned on those who'd held her, bringing the stick around to smack the first one in the head. He went down, hands raised to ward off more blows. But she couldn't stop. She beat him again and again until there was nothing but red streaming from his crushed head. Her fingers shook, then surged with power, and she turned on the second one, screaming in rage as she raised the stick once, twice, thrice. Curses flew from her lips. Then she stopped. The child. She needed to save the child. Bright flames filled the air as she turned, moving past the broken stone walls to where the soldiers were dragging the screaming child . . .

The vision blurred, but the fear remained, real, hard, and red-hot. Something twisted in her belly and a sickness came over her. Her neck burned. The strength faded from her arms, and then she was back in the Dungeon of the Damned. This time she was tied up, unable to move or fight. She shook from the cold, the horrific screams echoing off the walls, and the deep musk of fear. Her shoulders shook, begging for freedom, but she was trapped by inaction. Her nemesis. She wanted to be out, acting, fighting, running, anything but this restrictive imprisonment. She opened her mouth and a scream wailed out of her throat, long, mournful, and heartbroken.

"Maeve!" someone called in the distance, but they seemed so far away. "Maeve! Wake up! It's only a dream. A nightmare. Wake up!"

Maeve opened her eyes, red-rimmed and glassy. Her neck ached from the awkward angle she'd slept in. When she looked up, the unexpected gaze of one of the pirates met hers. It was the younger one. Imer. He stood in the open space where the iron grating had been, staring at her. There was a darkness in his deep eyes, and a hardness. The glint of teasing was gone; all he did was stare, and a dark shudder went through Maeve. Something twisted in the pit of her belly, something dark and unexpected. A flush rose to her cheeks, and she struggled upward, fingers fumbling for the rope to take it apart.

"Maeve?" Caspian's steady voice broke the strange moment between her and Imer. "Are you all right?"

His fingers came to touch her arm, gentle, and yet Maeve shrunk away. She was a hardened warrior and did not succumb to feelings. She was self-sufficient, steady; she could handle herself. Although she appreciated Caspian's help, she did not want it when it came to her nightmares. Her thoughts flickered back. The dream. What was it? There was a ring of familiarity to it, but why? Because she'd had it more than once? But it somehow felt more intense than it had been in the Sea of Sorrows.

"I'm fine," she whispered, letting go of the rope. She met his gaze. "Are we there?"

Sandrine's voice rang out as she said, "Come along. Are you going to sit here all night?"

Keeping her focus on Imer, Maeve rose, somewhat unsteadily. Her hands reached out for the curved walls, fingers gripping barnacles and other sea-grown weeds as she swayed in place. Her legs shook, giving her the sense that they would not hold her up for long. Curses rose to her lips. Oh, by the Divine, why couldn't she walk? Especially with that horrid pirate looking on.

Sandrine smirked from behind Imer, then turned and gingerly made her way down the jelly-lit hall.

Maeve realized Caspian was in the same situation. He stood in place with his arms spread out, balancing himself, a deep frown marring his handsome face.

A wave of nausea rode Maeve, a mix of the rolling feeling and the bitter taste of her nightmare.

"Draconbane awaits," Imer said, his lip curling as the words left his lips. He spoke as if in jest, but there was a tightness in his face.

Maeve refused to glance at him again, even though she addressed him. "How long did it take?" she asked, more to adjust herself to what she'd see outside.

Imer folded his arms. "Last night and most of the day. We'll be in full view of the dragons, if there are any left." He snorted to himself, but his earlier joviality was gone.

Caspian began to pace back and forth, checking his footing. "You will return our weapons to us." It was less of a question and more of a request.

Imer smirked. "Follow the path. My brother shall return them to you."

Maeve's eyes narrowed, wondering what Sandrine had in store for them. The questions of last night lay thick on her tongue. She wanted—needed—to know. Sandrine's method of dealing out information piecemeal was not enough. She needed to know as much as possible to have a hope of stopping the fae. Being locked in a cell with Sandrine had done nothing to loosen the tongue of the older woman, and Maeve bit her lip in frustration. Instead of sleeping, she should have pressed Sandrine for information. The key was in the book; it had to be. Perhaps she could steal it from Sandrine; she just had to make a plan with Caspian and take action.

"Maeve, are you coming?" Caspian's concerned voice floated to her ears.

Glancing up at him, she nodded, loosening her hold on the walls. "Go ahead." She gave him a small reassuring smile. "I'll be right behind you."

Caspian hesitated, then moved past Imer, out of the cell. Maeve watched his body language, his shoulders high and tight, his mouth set in a grim line as he stepped around the pirate, staying as far away as possible from him. Maeve cocked her head and took a step, relieved to find that her balance was back. When she had a moment alone with Caspian, she'd ask him what happened with him and the brothers. Whatever it was, it took place before she'd started working for him.

She kept walking until she was close to Imer. The iron grating hadn't been raised all the way, and she had to duck under as she walked out of the room. A hand came up, touching her bare arm, and she flinched, surprised to find Imer right next to her. He was a few inches taller than her with a slim, fit body and eyes like motes of light. They were so close she felt the heat of his body and saw the flecks of gold in his eyes. He lifted a hand, and she noticed that his fingers were long, slim, almost elegant, as though he did not use his hands for labor. She supposed from the odd shape of the boat, that could be true. He seemed a thinker, more willing to use his mind than his brute strength. Something inside her ached just from standing beside him, and an instinctual awareness rose. She pulled her arm away and glared at him. "Don't touch me," she whispered.

He responded with a quirk of his brow and answered in a low tone, "You're one of them. Aren't you?"

Maeve's guard went up and questions danced through her mind. What did he know? How much had Sandrine told him? Did he and his brother know about the fae? The quest? An uneasiness crept up her spine, and she shivered, swallowed, and answered, "One of who?"

His gaze was riveted on the ruby of her crown, and then his eyes swept down, resting on her collarbone, shoulders, and then breasts. "There are markings on your skin, aren't there?"

Maeve froze. "How did you know?" She racked her mind, thinking of past encounters. "Have we met before?"

The teasing grin came again, and he pulled back, his mischievous mask covering the former intensity of his stare. "I should say not. I'd remember if I'd met you before." He gave her a flirtatious wink. "Nay, you must be one of the lost Carnites."

Maeve's next words caught in her throat. Carn. No one talked about Carn, and none other than the fae had thrown that in her face. A sudden longing to know her history and to understand who her people were rose. It wasn't important, was it? The past was the past, but he'd brought it up.

Her fingers gripped his wrist, and now it was her turn to move closer. "What do you know about Carn?"

He pulled away as smoothly as an eel. "That knowledge will cost you," he said with a laugh, then started down the path, following in Caspian's wake.

Irritation sparked through Maeve, and she stared after him, at a loss on how to respond.

18

SHORE OF DRACONBANE

When they reached the end of the passage, the gangway to the strange boat lay open. Imer motioned to the chest, and Maeve bent to retrieve her weapons, grateful for the cold steel in her hands once again. A vibration went through her body, embers of a fire, a desire for a challenge, for an opportunity to wield her sword in battle once more. As she walked down the gangplank her eyes adjusted to the dim light. Evening shadows covered the shore, and other than the flickering torches Sandrine and the other pirate, Ingram, held, there was no light. Maeve's sandaled feet touched down on grit, something thicker than sand, likely a twisted bed of rocks and sticks, but it was difficult to see.

Behind her was the sea, the gentle waves lapping

peacefully against the shore, and she wondered if the strange boat had bumped up against the eels of the sea as they traveled. It seemed an effortless trip, aside from the rocking, though it still felt like the ground was shifting under her. She turned slowly, taking in the vague lumps of something in the distance. Hills? Mountains? It was too dark to tell. She opened her mouth to speak, but Sandrine was faster.

"Right then, it's not ideal to spend too much time by the shore. We need to head directly inland and find a place to take shelter. At first light, we take in our surroundings and head toward the mountains."

Maeve froze, dread sweeping through her. She crossed her arms over her chest as a scowl came to her face. "What do you mean, we?" she demanded.

Sandrine gave her a penetrating stare. "Yes, we," she confirmed, her voice flat. "We are in Draconbane, one of the most dangerous places known to us. If, by chance, we come across dragons in our quest, the brothers are the best chance we have against them. Besides, you said you need warriors to assist you in your quest. Now you have three."

Irritation sparked through Maeve. Three warriors. Caspian, Ingram, and Imer? She could almost feel the vibration of Caspian's anger, forced to travel into certain death with two brothers he despised, and the unfriendliness of the pirates was unfortunate. There was no trust between them, and all warriors knew it was best to perform a task like this with someone you could trust, who would have your back should things go wrong. With present company, Maeve was worried about being stabbed in the back before she could find the next shard.

She stepped back and motioned to Sandrine. "May I have a word with you? Alone?"

Sandrine's lips turned up into a smirk, and she handed her torch to Caspian and pointed toward the ship. "Back inside to the glowing halls. It's the only place for privacy, if you wish it."

Maeve backed up the gangplank, fury washing over her in waves. She took deep breaths to calm herself, and once the others were out of view, she whirled on Sandrine. "Why didn't you tell me about the pirates? If I had known they were coming with us . . ." she trailed off sharply, unsure what she would have done if she'd known in advance. Surely she wouldn't have included Caspian. Or at least told him, so he could have made a more informed decision. She wanted him with her, and yet confusion twisted through her.

Sandrine rested her hands on her hips. "You what? Wouldn't have included that warlord? Caspian? Like I said before, I will tell you what you need to know about this quest when you need to know it. For now, we are going to the mountains, and you need ruthless warriors on your side. There are fearsome creatures here, and I intend to stay alive. Ignore the brothers if you wish. They will guard me, and you can fend for yourself. But I warn you, should this quest go wrong, you will have the fae to answer to, as will I."

Maeve frowned, feeling trapped once again. "Not if I'm dead," she muttered.

"That would be your own fault," Sandrine snapped. "I did not invite you to bring a warlord who has a problem with my hired help. If they erupt into fighting, just remember: I warned you. He should not have come, regardless of how much gold you're paying him."

Maeve bit her lip. "Why did the pirates agree to this? Surely there's nothing in it for them?"

Sandrine shook her head. "This conversation is over. What you don't understand is that people have motives, needs. Once you understand them, it's easy to manipulate them. That's why I'm a scholar and you're a warrior. Because I know how to use my head and not just beastly violence. Now, come. If you don't want to talk to the brothers, walk in the back, but keep your complaints to yourself."

With that, Sandrine turned and left the ship, leaving Maeve fuming.

Maeve spun on her heel and followed Sandrine back down to the group. Tension lay thick in the air, and she felt like she could reach out and touch the line of animosity between Caspian and the pirates. Frowning, she fell into step with him while Sandrine took the lead with the brothers.

"How did it go?" he whispered.

Maeve shrugged. "Apparently she hired them before

I ran into you. She's shrewd and thinks ahead, that's for sure. She knew we were coming here, to Draconbane, and decided I might need help. I'm sorry. I did not know before I dragged you into this."

Caspian set a heavy hand on her shoulder and squeezed. "It's not your fault; don't hold that over your head. I'm here because I want to be by your side and help you through this."

That last remark should have made her feel warm instead of wary. She couldn't lay a finger on why, though, so she dismissed her anxious feelings. Caspian wanted to help, and the fact that she didn't fully understand why didn't mean she shouldn't trust him.

She shrugged his hand off her shoulder. "What's with you and the pirates? Why don't you get along? What did they do to you?"

Caspian went quiet, and even though it was too dark to see his expression, Maeve felt him close down and turn inward. She sensed his hesitation, and then he stopped walking, his eyes on the flickering torchlight ahead.

Sandrine and the pirate brothers set a quick pace through the darkness, as though they knew the land. The wind off the sea blew cold, and Maeve rubbed her arms as she stood there with Caspian, watching Sandrine and the brothers move farther inland.

Caspian waited just a beat longer and then began to walk, moving the torch he held from one hand to the other. "It happened a few years back," he began, his voice so soft the lull of the waves almost washed it away. "Three, maybe four years ago, during a heist for a high-profile warlord. It was back in the days when nothing mattered"—his voice went husky and then hard with regret—"except winning, being the best. We raided a temple for a holy relic and it went bad. It was my first heist with the brothers, Ingram and Imer. I should have known better; I should have used my own men, like I always do. When there's trust . . . there has to be trust among thieves. We didn't see ourselves as thieves back then, but that's what we were, taking what didn't belong to us for profit. Sometimes it was for the right reasons, but most of the time it was for the wrong ones."

A cold dread snaked along Maeve's spine. She spoke up, steering Caspian back to the story, back to what happened. "A holy relic? What was it?"

"Nothing unusual. It was a statue made of gold, decorated with gems. A replica of a divine being. I don't recall which one, but it was worth five hundred golden coins. Our goal was to retrieve it, leave the temple undisturbed, and take the item to a collector who would pay us well for speed and secrecy. After we snuck in, we discovered we had bad information; the relic was not where we were told it would be. Ingram offered to capture one of the priestesses to assist us. I was against it, but they overruled me. Ingram snatched one and his charms were effective, too effective. She became enamored and begged him to take her with him. After we found the relic, we headed for the location we'd stashed our horses in, and Ingram and Imer attacked me. It had never been their intent to include me in the deal. They took the treasure, the priestess, and headed off for who knows where. I still have the scar."

Maeve almost stumbled, stunned. "You never told me about this."

"There are many adventures that went wrong, and I haven't shared them all with you," Caspian said. "There is much about your past I don't know either."

Maeve glanced over at him, but his face hid in shadows. Maeve chewed her lips, at a loss for words. She recalled her transgressions of the past, the things she'd done that had likely led others to hold a grudge against her. If the Divine heard her prayers, regardless of what she'd done, couldn't the same be true for the pirate brothers? She was in an impossible situation. She didn't trust the brothers, and yet she had to trust them, and Sandrine. If they did not keep their word, follow through, she had nothing. She'd be locked up in the Dungeon of the Damned and the fae would have their way with her. Even worse, Caspian was wrapped up in the mess too, and could end up paying the price if they were betrayed. Again. She shuddered, unsure whether that meant torture or something else. Her fingertips touched her neck, tracing the line of the collar. Heat flared against her fingers, and again she recalled the Master explaining her fate.

Rage ripped through her belly and her fingers clenched into fists. There had to be a way to get free, to stop them. She couldn't be a pawn of the fae. Her strength thrashed inside her like a caged beast, fighting to get free. Resolve rose in her and she decided, come what may, she'd ask the pirate, traitor or not, what he knew about Carn. Perhaps the past held the key to unlocking her future.

19

ENCHANTED MISTS

THE HOWLS WOKE MAEVE; long, drawn-out mournful moans that made the hairs on her arms stand up straight and goosebumps pebble up and down her bare arms. She opened her eyes, surprised she'd slept at all with those unknown terrors keeping up noise throughout the night. There was something about those howls she could not explain, something that made her want to leave, return to the odd boat, and take her chances with the eels. The eels who had been silent throughout their sea journey.

Maeve rolled on her side, putting her back to the rear wall of the shallow cave they'd discovered a few miles off the coast. Sandrine had pressed forward relentlessly the evening before, determined to find a hiding place before the night terrors took over. Once they'd arrived, Sandrine told Maeve to sleep, while Caspian and the pirate brothers took turns keeping watch. Maeve had meant to wake up earlier and take a turn at keeping watch, but her sleep was dreamless and she slept later than she intended.

Her head felt dull and her muscles sore. She rose gingerly, shaking the stiffness out of her arms and legs. When she turned around, Imer was staring at her. He'd leaned up casually against the entrance to the cave, arms crossed, dark hair covered with his hat and one boot tapping against stone as he waited. Past him, she had a view of the gray mist, which hung like a cloud suspended in the air, so thick it was impossible to tell where the mist ended and the sea began. She shuddered, both at the look in Imer's dark eyes and the unfriendliness of the mountains.

Caspian walked over to Maeve, blocking Imer's view. A spark of irritation flared, but when Maeve met his eyes, something inside of her relaxed. Caspian was safe; she trusted him, but she also did not understand why she felt conflicted. Her eyes flickered ever so briefly back to Imer, but he'd turned to address his brother, their low tones adding warmth to the coolness of the cave.

Caspian touched her arm briefly. "Are you ready?"

Maeve shrugged, then crossed her arms. "Yesterday, when we were leaving the boat, Imer said something about Carn, my homeland. I need to talk to him. I want to know what he knows about my land of birth, my people."

Caspian scrubbed a hand over his stubble, his jaw set tight. "After what I told you last night, you still want to speak with them?"

Maeve blinked, realizing he was forcing her to choose a side. "There is no harm in talking to a pirate. Remember why we're here—to gain knowledge, not hold on to old grudges. If he knows something about Carn, something that might help me, I need to find out what it is."

Caspian's expression gentled in light of her rebuke. "Forgive me if I am overprotective of you. I took my eyes off you once, and the fae stepped in and did this to you." He gestured to the collar. "My past dealings with the brothers make me want to strike them down, but I will hold off. For now."

Maeve opened her mouth, unsure of what to say. Caspian's words confused her, as did his grudge. When they were in the outpost, he'd talked about the Divine, but now he wanted vengeance on his old enemies. She supposed it made sense. If she were in his place, her desire for revenge would be the same. Again, she wished she were privy to Sandrine's plans; that would change everything.

Her eyes tore across the rough walls of the sloping cave. "Where's Sandrine?" she asked, whirling toward the pirates.

Ingram scowled and spat, then jerked his chin toward the mist.

"She's out there?" Maeve clarified. "In the mist?

Alone?" She marched to the entrance, glaring at the brothers in turn. "And she hired you to be her protectors."

Imer snorted, a grin coming to his lips at her outburst. "You'll soon come to learn that she knows best. Besides, she's out there mapping our journey."

As Maeve brushed by Imer, his fingers touched her arm. They were warm and sent something like a shock rippling through her. "Find me sometime," he whispered, "and I'll tell you what I know about Carn. For a price."

Maeve's cheeks burned as she slipped out into the mist. He had her. He knew what she wanted and yet, as always, there was a price. She recalled the gold she'd taken from the warlord's keep. Would some of it be enough to keep him happy? He was a pirate after all, or at least masquerading as one. There was something odd about the two brothers, something she couldn't quite wrap her mind around, but thoughts of them disappeared as she stepped outside.

The whiteness hid the world from view, wrapping around her face like a cold and clammy hand. Then it faded, circling around Maeve as though she'd stepped into a portal and the light inside recognized her. A sensation of wonder filled her, and the eerie howling that had woken her faded away.

"You feel it too, don't you?" Sandrine said.

Mist circled around Sandrine like a whirlpool. She

stood tall with her book open in both hands, her gaze riveted to it.

"What is it?" Maeve breathed.

"Enchanted mist," Sandrine said. "It is meant to guard this place and keep people out, I suppose. But if you know how to walk through it, like I do, you can see it for what it is."

Maeve studied her. "You're more than a scholar, aren't you? You're a healer too, and you know how to handle enchanted mists. I'm curious, what other powers do you have? Will you ever tell me your tale?"

The lines on Sandrine's face softened and her tone was almost gentle. "There is nothing to tell, girl. Not until we get out of here. I've found the remnants of the road we must follow. The mist will hide us for some time, but then we'll be out in the open. The Divine help us then. There are many foul rumors of what lies out here, but we will discover the truth. And the shard."

There was a glint in her eyes, and Maeve had the slightest sense that Sandrine was enjoying herself.

"Will you tell me more?" she pressed. "Which mountain range do we need to go up to? I know you said you'd tell me what I need to know when I need to know it, but what if something happens to you? Divine forbid it, and you have the brothers to protect you, but I must know what to do should I need to continue this quest alone."

The book slammed shut in Sandrine's hands so hard an inch of dust came off it. She glared at Maeve, and her voice was low as she said, "Failure is not an option. If anything happens to me, Maeve of Carn, the quest shall end and you'll be a pawn of the fae. If I face death, you will face it with me, or answer to the fae. And who knows what they will do with the likes of you. Besides, there is no guarantee they will ever set you free, even if you finish this quest for them."

Maeve wilted under Sandrine's fury, frustrated by the reminder of her complete and utter helplessness. She spun on her heel, throwing her next words over her shoulder. "I'll keep that in mind, just as I'll keep in mind the fact that dragons might be alive."

Sandrine said nothing in response.

20

MOUNTAIN SLOPES

THE NEXT WEEK was frustrating for Maeve. Sandrine stonewalled her, refusing to share her knowledge and keeping the book hidden at all times. Even Caspian's charms did nothing to thaw the scholar's icy resolve. The brothers seemed nothing more than silent shadows. They kept to themselves when the group made camp and spoke to each other in low tones. Every now and then she saw Ingram drink from a pouch and wondered if it was his secret supply of liquor. Imer did not seem keen on drink, but he was restless and seemed unable to stand or sit still for long. It seemed like he never slept. He was pacing when Maeve went to sleep, and regardless of how early she woke, he was already up and dressed, with a finger on the hilt of his blade. More often than not, his dark eyes met hers and then drifted down, as though he could read the markings on her chest, hidden under her breastplate.

The silent attention made her feel both uncomfortable and desired. She'd had her fair share of dealing with men, but it had been a long time since a man made her feel wanted for more than her skills with the blade. That, added to his potential knowledge of the words inked across her chest, made her crave speaking with him again. Yet, despite her earlier conversation with Caspian, he always ended up in the way each time she had the opportunity to speak with Imer. While she trusted Caspian and valued his opinion, it was frustrating that he kept silently interfering. Was Caspian protecting her, or was he jealous of the looks Imer gave her? And then there was Imer himself. He hadn't made an attempt to speak with her again, always eyeing Caspian and moving away. But she couldn't forget the way his touch made her feel, for it was so different from Caspian's comforting presence. Why was that? Did she harbor some attraction toward Imer? But that was ridiculous, it was Caspian, had always been Caspian. In little more than a year Caspian was the one who'd been able to break through her defenses, encourage her to become part of a team, and fight together. Yet, just when she thought they might be something more, he'd thrown all that away for what? For a sacred path? Knowledge of the Divine?

One morning, she woke and tasted dust in the air. They'd camped near the slopes of a mountain range with gray peaks that shot up out of reach, some capped with snow far in the distance. The land was taking on some character, a change from the gritty brown landscape they'd passed day after day. Maeve sat up, taking in her surroundings. She hadn't expected to actually like the mountains, but there was something oddly surreal about their wild and craggy beauty. In some places, she could see for miles and miles, and it was intimidating; it gave her a feeling that the world might be much larger than she'd ever imagined.

They'd traveled directly east since landing on shore, and to the north she saw vague shapes, what looked like the ruin of a town. To the south there was nothing, although she thought she saw hints of green in the distance, though it could have been sunlight reflecting off the gray stones.

"This way," Sandrine called. She stood in a hollow between two mountains, where a flattened dirt path sloped upward like a secret, sneaking its way into the heart of the mountains. "It will be a long trek today."

Ingram took the lead, moving up the slope as though he'd done nothing but train to climb mountains his entire life. Maeve watched out of lidded eyes, curious about the brothers.

Who were they? Why had they built such an odd ship, and what did they want so badly that they would risk everything to join forces with Sandrine and lead a party into the dreaded Draconbane Mountains?

A shadow flickered over her face and she jumped,

heart pounding in her throat. Her eyes tore upward, and high above, a bird wheeled through the air. White feathers covered its wings, which had a span of at least twelve feet. One fell, drifting back and forth before it came to rest at Maeve's feet. Without thinking, she picked it up and tucked it into her belt. When she looked up, Imer was staring at her. Again.

"Go ahead, Caspian," she called out, her eyes not leaving Imer's rugged face. "I'll catch up."

Caspian grunted as he passed her, concern on his face, but he started up the mountain slope without looking back.

Maeve walked up to Imer, who cocked his head at her. That old, dangerous, flirtatious grin was back.

"Will you walk with me?" Maeve asked.

Imer touched two fingers to his hat. "We are traveling the same path, and I've never turned down an offer to walk with a fair lady."

Maeve scowled. "I'm a warrior, not a fair lady, and you'd do well to remember that."

"One can be both," he rejoined, "besides, I'm curious about you."

Maeve's fingers twitched, but she recovered in time to keep from punching him in his side. "Why the looks?" she asked, lowering her voice. "Why the stares, when you could have talked to me?"

"And risk angering your warlord friend? I think not." Imer grimaced in Caspian's direction.

The path was wide enough to allow them to walk

side by side up the slope. It flowed evenly, and soon the rocks were replaced with patches of light green grass that flattened under their footsteps. Uncanny silence hung like a threat in the air, like a trap waiting until its prey was in the proper place to release its fury. It was plain no humans had walked the path in a while.

"You know him from the past?" Maeve asked, trying to get some sense of the pirate's history.

"Aye." Imer touched his hat with two fingers again. "We've done a task or two together. Missions that always went wrong. He has some bitterness toward my brother and me, which I do not blame him for. We were in a difficult position, what was done needed to be done. But that is all in the past."

Maeve raised an eyebrow. Should she be surprised at his lack of apology? Or by the fact that he'd taken responsibility for his actions and admitted he did wrong by Caspian?

"Are you saying that to gain my trust?"

Imer smiled, but it did not reach his eyes. "Nay, fair lady. I would not try to gain your trust so quickly; I have done nothing to earn it. Besides, I am here to offer an exchange, knowledge for knowledge, nothing more."

Fair lady. Maeve wished he'd stop calling her that. "Speak plainly," she demanded, frustrated with his words and the mixed emotions he stirred up within her. "What do I have that you want?"

Imer gestured ahead to Sandrine. "The scholar. She gave us a compelling offer, one we could not refuse. But

I know it's only a cover for why we are truly here. Adventurers come here from time to time to dig up what jewels they can find along the shore. So, we've been here before; it's a lucrative endeavor, ferrying people across the Sea of Eels. Plus, the eels catch a fair price in the marketplace. But no one has asked for an escort into the heart of the mountains."

Maeve went still, wary. Why did Imer want to know the truth? Would it frighten him away or make him even more interested in the quest? Again, she recalled Caspian's tale. The brothers had stolen a holy relic—and a priestess—but she was more interested in the part about the relic. If they had an interest in holy relics, the shards would greatly interest them, if only for the price they could catch at the market rather than their ability to break all curses. How much truth should she give him?

She turned from his watchful gaze and shrugged. "There is not much to share. Sandrine and I are bound by a monster who sent us to retrieve an item for him. Once the quest is complete, he will return what has been stolen from us."

"Curious," Imer said, but his light tone showed he did not believe her. "Quite a story to tell. And what was taken from you that is so precious you're willing to risk life and limb?"

Maeve's fists clenched and her feet came down hard on the path. She quickened her pace, growling, "My freedom and my strength."

"Ah," Imer said, his voice gentling. "See, that wasn't

so hard. I would ask who your master is, but I believe I have an idea."

Maeve's eyebrows shot up, and she spun around, coming to a complete stop. "Who?" How many people knew about the fae and their growing influence?

Imer stepped in front of her, so close she had to tilt her head to see up into his gold-flecked eyes. Instead of the distant hardness she expected to see, there was a gentleness, a caring in his gaze. His hands came up to rest on her bare shoulders, his light touch making her shiver and crave more. A headiness came over her, like nothing she'd felt before, and involuntarily she leaned into the spell he cast over her. Who was he, this mysterious man that awakened things within her that shouldn't be awakened?

The warrior in her faded away, replaced with the lost youth of long ago, before she was hardened by the world and learned how to fight. Her eyes closed and her head fell back as a light wind played with loose strands of her hair. Warm hands drifted down her shoulders, touching the light brown runes on her skin. Her heart pounded in her chest, so hard she thought he must hear it, and a flush rose from her neck.

"May I see?" he whispered.

He smelled like the sea, wild and free, eager to go wherever it wished, do whatever it wanted. Like freedom. If she kissed him, would he taste like salt and sunshine?

What hold did he have on her? What madness? For

she was giving in at just his touch, at the unexpected gentleness of his words. A desperate desire thrummed through her body to have more of his warmth, to envelop herself in him and forget about the quest, the fae, and the potential of dragons.

"Yes," she whispered.

His fingers undid the laces of her sheath, baring her upper chest down to where her breastplate covered her breasts and stomach. A lump settled in her throat as his fingers brushed against the swirls that decorated her collarbone.

"They are beautiful," he breathed, a light in his eyes, lost in awe. "Do you know what the runes mean?"

Maeve shook her head. "I know nothing of Carn, my people, or my parents. It was all lost so long ago."

His brow furrowed. "Do you recall anything? Do you remember those early days before it all went to ruin?"

Maeve could not meet his eyes. "Nay, there is nothing."

But even as she said the words, she recalled suppressed emotions. Fear. Terror. Heat. Pain. And screams of death. Her nightmare from the Sea of Sorrows came back, the sensation hitting her so hard she hissed and recoiled from Imer's touch.

"What is it?" he asked, his voice distant.

There was a keen howl, and then a terrifying scream filled the air.

Maeve jerked out of her reverie, her hands flying to her sword. "Did you hear that?"

Imer turned in the direction the others had disappeared in. "Sounds like trouble."

Bloodlust surged through her, and all thoughts of Carn and dark nightmares disappeared. Maeve drew her blade and dashed up the slope, with Imer right behind her.

21

BANSHEE SCREAMS

THE PATH BECAME steep then jerked sharply, weaving back and forth into higher peaks. Cliffs loomed up on either side like stone monsters leaning over to capture their prey. Then they backed off, giving way to an open plain. A raw wind blew through the plain, bringing smells of dirt, old rot, death, and danger.

Maeve came to a standstill, buffeted by the wind at her back. She examined the grass, noting the trail of crimson blood leading toward a darkness in the mountainside that rose on her left. A hole? A cave? Something else? It was too dark to tell, but the matted blood led that way.

On her right, a gentle hill sloped upward and opened up into a valley with a breathtaking view of how high they'd come. A lake glistened in the distance and hills and valleys turned into slopes of the lower mountain peaks. Farther away, she saw white peaks glinting in the sunlight.

"Something attacked them." Imer, barely winded from their run uphill, pointed at the blood. His voice was full of concern. "They could be hiding, or whatever it was could be waiting to attack us."

As if confirming his words, another scream sounded, low and wild, the cry of a feral creature. Maeve's blood went cold, and for a moment she was back in the dungeon, where the banshees screamed. No—impossible. But she knew, deep in her heart, that anything was possible in Draconbane.

Her hand shot out and closed around Imer's upper arm, pulling him back. A fiery bolt of power shot through her, preparing her for action, and her fingers squeezed the hilt of her sword, a familiar comfort. She was strong, she could fight, and fighting was better than hunting for lost relics or attempting to remember her shrouded past.

"Imer, I've heard that kind of scream before. I believe it's a banshee. If so, we must tread carefully. They are merciless, and if it has captured our friends . . ."

Caspian. Was he all right? He was stronger than her, now that her strength was collared, and almost as good as she was with a blade. She could count on him to know what to do. The unknowns were Sandrine and Ingram. How would they handle an attack?

"A banshee? Are you sure?" Imer took a step back, glancing from her to the hidden recess.

"I'll lead the way." Maeve stepped in front of him.

"It is unnecessary, fair lady," he said, keeping stride with her.

"Please stop calling me fair lady," Maeve groaned. "I am no damsel in distress."

She caught the edge of his smile as a flirtatious grin spread across his face. "Aye, you are a damsel in distress, a lady with no knowledge of home, but knowledge of dark creatures such as banshees. Pray tell, how does one slay a banshee?"

Maeve bit her tongue and swung her sword. "Banshees are spirits. There is no way to slay them. We have to outwit it and slay whatever monster it works for."

"Monster? Are they not free beings?"

Maeve followed the blood trail, narrowing her eyes. Her next words came out a low whisper. "From what I've heard, most are bound to monsters who use them as a lure."

"I know the tales," Imer rejoined. " *'When a banshee screams, your soul will rest in eternal dreams'*."

Maeve wished he had not uttered those words. Slightly frustrated, she waved her hand at him, motioning for him to stay silent as they crept nearer to the darkness. The mountainside curved inward on itself, creating a yawning mouth that sloped downhill. Maeve paused at the entrance of the cave, letting her eyes adjust to the dim light. She listened, but there was nothing aside from the odd drip of water. The scream had gone, and while the trail of red continued into the gloom, she could not see nor hear her comrades. She glanced at Imer, then recalled he was not familiar with raiding a place, nor did he know her habits. Caspian's unfortunate tale came to the forefront of her mind, although she had some trouble believing that Imer would double-cross her. In fact, he seemed more interested in her heritage than she was. Besides, his brother was missing, and so she set aside her concerns about him attacking her.

As soon as she stepped into the cave, her senses were assaulted with the pungent smell of decay. Something had died recently, and its flesh was rotting and moldering in the cave. She pressed her free arm in front of her mouth while her eyes watered from the stink.

There was a rustle of wind, a low wail, and then, materializing out of the deepness of the cave, came a woman. She had long hair, wild and matted, that fell to her knees, and her bone-thin body was covered with dirty rags that swept the floor. Her face was hidden in the gloom, but she reached out toward Maeve and Imer. "Help me," she groaned. "Please. Help me."

Maeve hissed, and before Imer could step forward and gallantly offer to help, she pointed her sword toward the woman. "Who are you? Where are my friends?"

The woman shook her hands, lowered her head, and moaned again. "Help me. *Please*. Help me."

Her voice echoed in the cave, sending chills up

Maeve's spine. She swallowed the lump in her throat, briefly closed her eyes, then dashed forward.

Imer let out a shout at her unexpected move, but it did not slow Maeve. She pointed her sword at the woman's chest and ran it through her heart.

Nothing happened. The spectral form remained frozen in place, but then the woman's body began to flicker. She pointed a finger at Maeve as she threw off her rags. A scream came from her lips, wild, frantic, and feral. The creature spun and hurled a violent windstorm toward Maeve, who lost her balance and fell.

Imer shouted again and rushed forward to attack the creature, but the spectral woman vanished, leaving them alone in the cave.

"Divine save us," Imer muttered, wiping a hand over his head. "She's the banshee."

"Come on." Maeve beckoned, moving farther into the cave.

No sooner had the words left her mouth than a roar thundered from deep inside the cave.

Her fingers tightened around her sword and she moved faster, her feet crunching rocks and shaking stones loose. They tumbled and scattered around her. The walls loomed higher as she moved farther in, and the natural dimness of the cave grew nearly pitch-black. Maeve cast about for a light and, coming up empty-handed, finally paused and glanced back at Imer.

His jaw was tight, but even in the shadows she saw determination on his face coupled with a surprising calmness. He held a short sword in his right hand and in his left was an orb-like object that glowed. It appeared to be the same jellylike substance they'd had in the boat.

Maeve opened her mouth to say something, but his gaze met hers. "I'll lead the way," he said, and the tone of his voice warned her against arguing with him.

Maeve followed Imer as the tunnel sloped down. She placed one hand on the wall to brace herself and took quick, tiny steps. The roar came again, but this time she also heard steel clanging against rock. Fighting. Heart in her throat, she quickened her pace. Caspian. He needed her help.

The tunnel leveled out and curved sharply, hurling them into a cavern lit by flickering torchlight. In the middle of it was a bearlike beast. It reared up on its hind legs, reaching almost ten feet in height as it roared. Claws the size of Maeve's face slashed the air, coming dangerously close to Caspian and Ingram, who danced around the beast, taking turns slashing at it. The beast had a mane of shaggy brown hair, similar to a lion's. It foamed at the mouth as it fought, and its red eyes were unfocused, rolling around in anger as it snarled and slashed.

Maeve took a step back in alarm, almost bumping into Imer, who stood at her elbow. But it wasn't the beast that surprised her—it was Sandrine. The scholar was kneeling in a corner of the cavern, her back to the chaos, digging in a pile of rocks. She moved slowly and methodically, as if there was not a monster in the cave that could kill her.

The smell of death hung in the air. Out of the corner of her eye, Maeve saw a pile of bones, some with meat still on them. It was the carcass of a large—very large—animal. She shuddered. What else lived up here in the mountains? What other creatures would they run into?

She blocked the thought from her mind and returned her focus to the beast. Caspian and Ingram were doing a valiant job of distracting it, but the beast was too wild, too unpredictable for them to get close enough to kill it. If she could sneak up behind it and stab it in the back, the four of them would have a chance at taking it down.

It seemed Imer read her mind, or at least had the same intention. He moved to the left, holding his short sword in both hands. There was a tightness in his face and his eyes were wary, a sign he wasn't used to fighting in close quarters. Or perhaps with a blade. Maeve forced her eyes back to the beast, although she was curious about Imer's actions. When she first met him, she assumed he spent his time fighting and causing chaos, but the reluctance to fight now wasn't fear, it was something else. What was it?

The beast roared again, sending a fire of boldness up Maeve's spine. Her feet pounded the stone ground as she ran, then pushed off with her toes and leaped. In a moment, she was airborne. She whipped her sword around, aiming it between the shoulder blades of the beast. The sword sunk into flesh, going so deep Maeve thought it would come out the other end. The beast gave a low howl, first in rage, then it tampered off to a pitiful moan. It staggered in place before falling forward, its weight creating a cloud of dust as it hit the floor of the cave.

Maeve allowed the momentum of the beast to carry her forward until she was standing on its back. With one hand, she yanked her sword clean and wiped off the bloody blade on the creature's fur before meeting the eyes assessing her.

Caspian gave her an encouraging nod and dropped his sword arm. Ingram's lips thinned as he gazed from her to the beast, and then he spun around, heading in the direction they'd come from. He grunted, "Doubtless there are more around here."

Imer joined him, leaving Caspian and Maeve to guard Sandrine.

"What are you doing down here?" Maeve asked through gritted teeth, glaring in Sandrine's direction. Would the scholar ever be open with her?

"Got it," Sandrine announced and rose gracefully, as though there hadn't just been a battle to the death. She held something firmly in her right fist and moved toward the brothers.

"What is it?" Maeve repeated her question, even more frustrated at being ignored. Her heart thumped hard in her chest. Just when she thought her friends were in mortal danger, it turned out to be nothing. The stream of blood she'd seen earlier was likely from a dead animal, the latest kill of the beast.

In a surprising move, Sandrine pivoted and faced her, a calmness in her eyes. "It's a spell, the lure we need to find the lair in the Draconbane Mountains."

She held up the object, and questions poured into Maeve's mind. How did the scholar know these things? What else was she hiding? And when would she let down her guard so Maeve could get her hands on the book?

22

ELUSIVE DARKNESS

NO MATTER how much Maeve pressed, Sandrine would not describe the object she'd found in the cave. Maeve had to accept that Sandrine knew what she was doing, and yet, as they traveled higher into the mountains, day after day, her frustration grew. Caspian was a friendly companion, but he was always on edge, always looking for battle and keeping an eye on the brothers. It was Ingram and Imer who Maeve was most curious about, and yet she felt reproached for her attraction to them. Caspian's cool gaze kept her away, and even Imer seemed to have withdrawn into himself, occasionally flashing her a flirtatious grin, one she came to know was a mask he wore to hide his true self.

The weather was extreme in the mountains. Even though it was late summer, the days were long and relentlessly hot. At night a chill swept over the mountain peaks, sometimes hidden in mist that stretched like fingers, reaching out to enwrap those who dared enter its vicinity. Maeve grew restless, and even when they found some shelter to bed down in, a sense of impending doom hung over her. There was something dark in the mountains, maybe a spirit or lost souls crying out, seeking vengeance. She didn't know what it was, but the darkness was almost palpable, and yet somehow elusive. Each time she tried to put a finger on what was niggling at her, it slipped away.

And then there were the nightmares. Over and over, she was the mother, desperate to save her child from the soldiers, the fire, and each time she dreamed, it became more real, frightening, terrifying, as though she were looking in a mirror, back into her past, back into the forgotten things that haunted her, things she had desperately tried to forget. Destruction. Fire. Bloodshed. Was there something symbolic there that she was missing? A message, a knowing, something that could help her escape from her prison?

The days ticked by, one after the other, and as Maeve walked uphill, her thighs sore, she realized the night of the full moon was less than ten days away. The Master planned to send a messenger to retrieve the shards during the full moon, and she was no closer to finding out how to evade them or escape the golden collar around her neck. Time was running short, and she did not have a plan.

"Hold," Ingram called from ahead.

He often led the way, with Sandrine correcting his path from time to time. They stood in the open near the granite peaks, and even though Sandrine had a spell that protected them from unseeing eyes, she couldn't help but wonder what hell would break loose in the mountain ranges if they were discovered by whatever lived here.

"What do you see?" Sandrine stood at his side and shielded her eyes with her hand, as though the added shade would give her eagle eyes.

Imer walked up on her other side and crossed his arms over his chest, as though his very appearance could drive horrors away.

Caspian moved to another boulder and peered out into the valley. Maeve joined him. Her hand went to her heart, and she took a breath of surprise as her blue eyes took in her surroundings. The tales she'd heard of the Draconbane Mountains had led her to assume it would be a cruel place, ridden with ashes, brown and barren, with sand blowing across the burned plains. But what she saw was no dark and deathly valley full of monsters, nor an impassable landscape; instead, she saw green grass and white flowers covering the slopes, their petals blowing in the ongoing mountain breeze.

There was something playful about the valley, and Maeve took a deep breath, tasting a hint of flower blossoms in the air, a sweetness, and something else. Her brow creased. It was tangy, salty, but unlike sea air. No, this was heat, fire, maybe ash. A warning made the hairs on her arm stand up, and the air felt electric. Her eyes scanned the valley again, trying to see what had made Ingram stop. Did he have the same vague sensation that all was not as it should be?

And then she smelled it. It was an old scent, rotten with layers of musk, like bodies pressed tight together day after day, rotting in their own filth. And yet they were alive, moving as one, a mountain of greed and desire, driving Maeve further into the darkness. The sensation came over her in a flash, and her fingers twitched. But no matter how hard she squinted her eyes, she could not see what it was, though her skin crawled with unease.

"Do you sense that?" she whispered to Caspian.

He glanced at her, his light hair ruffling in the breeze and thick arms crossed over his broad chest. The compassion in his eyes made her heart melt. How had she doubted him, her warlord, the one companion that made her feel completely at ease? A warmth washed over her, relief that he was there, with her, bearing the struggle together.

"I sense it, Maeve," he said as he frowned, unfolded his arms, and reached for his sword. "It's that darkness that's been following us since we stepped on the shore, the darkness Sandrine has hidden us from."

Maeve nodded. She'd thought as much, since she'd told Caspian about Sandrine having the ability to hide them within the enchanted mists.

"Either her strength has failed or we've come too far

into the mountains to hold it back any longer," he went on.

"It's been weeks," Maeve confirmed, discomfort riding her like a beast tamer rode the back of a wild horse, clinging so tight it was painful. "We should be close to finding the next shard, wherever it is hidden. I should have a word with Sandrine before whatever this is attacks us."

"Agreed." Caspian nodded. "It is coming for us, and whatever it is will be relentless. We are lucky to have stayed hidden for this long."

Maeve turned her body toward Caspian, feelings warring within her, words struggling to become coherent so she could speak them. She didn't know what it was, but there was something there, something she wanted to warn Caspian against. She didn't know why, and self-consciously she touched two fingers to the collar. "Caspian . . ."

His rough hand covered hers, pressing gently. "What is it?"

She shook her head, suddenly uncomfortable with their proximity. "I don't know . . . it's just . . ." She struggled for words, and then they came out in a rush. "The night of the full moon will be upon us soon, and I can't help but worry about Sandrine's warning. What if the fae come for you?"

Caspian shrugged, his jaw working. There was a darkness in his eyes, and a sadness too.

He sighed. "We've been over this. So what if they

do? What if they come for Ingram and Imer too?"

Maeve smirked. "You would like that, wouldn't you? But do you truly think the scholar would have hired them if she thought the fae would take them away?"

Caspian looked away, back out toward the valley. "I can't deny it would please me somewhat, but the past is the past. I should forgive them and move on."

Maeve shrugged. "I don't know what to think. The scholar plays a game of her own, and I cannot comprehend why she hired them. I spoke with Imer, weeks ago, but he's avoided me since. There's something he knows about Carn that he isn't saying, and I admit, I want to know. What if it helps with my past? With discovering the source of my extraordinary strength and knowing how to remove the collar?"

Caspian moved his hand to grip her upper arm, where runes rose on her skin, lost words and meanings. "Then you have to find out."

"Maybe if you stop glaring at him, I'll have a chance to find out," Maeve told him pointedly.

His voice lowered further. "Maeve, I have my grudge and my reasons, but if you are truly concerned about the fae, I can hide until the full moon is over with. They want the shards. That is all. When they get them, they will go back to what they were doing before."

"Hunting." Maeve stepped away, and a coldness went through her, like a mist from the sea wrapping its invisible arms around her bare shoulders. "They were one step ahead of me before, why should now be any different?"

"Have a little faith, Maeve," he said as he let her arm go. He paused, his eyes cloudy, and he looked away from her, chewing his lower lip as though deciding whether he should say more.

Maeve waited, but when nothing else was forthcoming, she nodded and walked away, surprised to see Sandrine had also turned away from the brothers and was striding in her direction. The two met in the middle, between the two boulders.

Maeve stood tall, looking down at the older woman, determined to be passive and not feed into her desperate need to know what was about to take place.

Sandrine opened her hand. A round, golden object lay in her palm. "Take it, girl," she said, holding it out toward Maeve.

There was something inside the object, pulsing with light. "What is it?" she asked, making no move to pick it up.

"The Finder's Stone. It is a tool used to find treasure. The closer you get to your goal, the warmer it becomes. It has led us true, for I believe the lair of dragons is beyond the valley. But once we are there, it will be too late to turn back, and my spells are failing. I don't have the strength to hide us any longer, and they will come for us."

"Who are they? What is coming?" Maeve whispered, barely daring to draw breath.

Sandrine glanced out at the valley, then back at Maeve. She leaned in closer, silver strands of hair falling out of her hastily made bun. "Goblins. Fierce little fighters with hearts for treasure. They are greedier than dragons, but were too frightened of them to take action when the mountains were alive with dragonkind. They will have taken up residence in the lair, and you must fight them. That's why I brought the brothers with us. They expect gold as payment, but they shall be lucky to escape with their lives."

Maeve swallowed hard as rage welled up within her. Was Sandrine double-crossing the pirates? Leading them to their deaths so she and Maeve could survive?

Words came out of her mouth before she could stop them. "What if we waited?"

Sandrine scowled. "Wait? Wait for what?"

"The night of the full moon," Maeve hurried on. "If there are goblins inside the dragon lair, then we need help. And if the fae are coming to take the last shard I found, then surely they will assist with driving away the goblins."

Sandrine scowled harder and her eyes turned dark. "Are you a fool, girl? They are our masters." She pointed at the collar around Maeve's neck. "If we wait until the night of the full moon to attack the goblins and the fae portal into the middle of a battlefield, they will believe we set them up for ambush. Do you want this quest to be called off? Do you want to rot forever in the Dungeon of the Damned?"

"Surely you don't think they would believe we set them up to be ambushed," Maeve pressed.

Sandrine took a step closer, almost poking a finger into Maeve's breastplate. "You don't know how dangerous they are. We do this the way I'm telling you, or I walk away and leave you and your warlord to die. The fae will find another way. They always have, and they always will. So, listen, and stop trying to deviate from the plan."

Maeve's temper rose. "It is not a plan, it's what *you* want *me* to do. Why won't you share anything with me until it's too late?"

"It's for your protection," Sandrine scoffed. "Now take this. Should worse come to worse, it will guide you to the next locations."

Questions rose on Maeve's tongue. "Where is the next location? How will this relic guide me? And how do you know about it?"

"Who do you think told me about this relic? Who had the time to spend days tracking it down?" Sandrine snapped. "The portals the fae use are not as potent as you assume. They can only open them on ground where blood has been spilled. There is much about them you don't know, so don't underestimate them, girl. The lost shards have a potent power, and they will stop at nothing to retrieve them. Why do you think they planned so carefully and chose you, specifically, to carry out their wishes? You may not know what they have on you, but I do. It is my duty to know the dark things, the hidden things, and there is a reason for everything that happens. The fae looked for something like you to help them, something with your strength and your abilities. They have done their research; they have searched this world in its entirety for exactly what they need. When the moonlight shines upon this world in full, the fae use their portals with a purpose, and they will not stand for trickery. If there was a way to take them down, I would have done so long ago."

Maeve's fury evaporated and her breath caught, torn between frustration and astonishment. "You would have taken them down? But . . ." she paused. How much could she trust Sandrine? "You work for them; how can I trust your word?"

Sandrine lifted her chin and thrust the oblong object into Maeve's hand. "I've said too much already. If things go wrong here in Draconbane, make sure you continue with the quest. There may yet be a chance for you. After you find the lost shard in the dragon's lair, head south toward the ruins of Carn."

Maeve froze, and everything within her screamed in rebellion. Carn? The lost ruins of her homeland? She'd never been there and with good reason. She had no desire to go back, to look on the scattered ruins of her people and knowledge that was lost to her forever. But returning to Carn might awaken old desires and bring her clarity. What if she could find knowledge that would free her from the collar? Her heart soared for a moment at the possibility of finding answers, but just as suddenly, her crown felt heavy on her head. Why did she wear it? What was the point? She was the queen of nothing, and her people were all dead. Gone.

"There's a lost shard? There?" she demanded in disbelief.

"Aye," Sandrine nodded. She turned, jerking her chin toward Ingram and Imer. "Why do you think I called on the pirates? They are fearsome warriors, but they also know about Carn. You should ask them what they know of its history when you have a chance."

"They know . . ." Maeve repeated, her fingers going to her lips. "You did this on purpose so I could learn more. Find out more." Her voice came out as a whisper. "Sandrine, what do you really know? Whose side are you on, because I am confused. At times you seem to speak out against the fae, and wish for their demise, and at other times, like these, it seems you're on my side, and you want me to win."

Sandrine's expression went blank, and she fixed Maeve with a fierce look. Holding up a finger, she spoke quickly, "Girl. Understand this now. I am on no one's side. I am too old for wars and betrayal and mistakes. The fae have me and I have nothing left other than to do as they wish. You'd better do the same until you find a way out. I'm just telling you what you need to know to survive, should things not go as planned."

Maeve pressed on, determined to get to the truth, "But you know what will happen. A horde of goblins will attack us as we search for treasure, and you expect that a few of us will die, and I must go on, complete the quest." Her fingers shook with frustration. "I don't like this any more than you do, but we are in this together. I hope. I pray."

Sandrine turned away. "Pray to the Divine if you must. The celestial beings have minds of their own, plans of their own, and I too hope they will stand up and defeat evil before it goes too far. In the meantime, think of what I have told you."

"Wait." Maeve stepped forward, her hand coming out to spin Sandrine around, but she drew it back at the last moment. For some reason, it seemed strange and wrong to touch the scholar even mildly violently. "What about this object, the Finder's Stone? How do I use it?"

Sandrine turned back and glanced at the oblong gold item. "Think on the item you desire, and it will lead you in the right direction. The pulsing lights will lead you straight and true until you find what you are looking for."

Maeve glanced down at her armor, looking for a place to keep the object. "It is curious," she admitted. "Why don't the fae have it?"

Sandrine fixed her with a look. "Do you think the fae could use such an object to find what they need in less than twelve hours of moonlight, twelve nights a year? Nay, they passed the knowledge to me."

Maeve understood. The fae used mortals for their plans. She took a step closer to Sandrine, extending the figurative olive branch. "Sandrine, if I ever find out anything that will free us from the fae, I will use it."

Sandrine stared at her, and although her face was still emotionless, there was a passion in her eyes. "That's what I'm counting on."

Maeve stood still, staring, as Sandrine returned to the pirates, her mind abuzz with thoughts. Sandrine had set this up to benefit her—the pirates, the Finder's Stone, everything—to help her destroy the fae. And yet, deep in her heart, she knew pieces of the dense puzzle were still missing.

She lifted her chin as she returned to Caspian's side. This time, when she looked down, she saw a sea of green, but not the green of grass nor the white of flowers swaying in the pleasant mountain breeze. Nay. The green was an off-color one, dirty and moldering, and it belonged to goblins with pointed ears and soiled loincloths moving toward Maeve and her companions.

Maeve's hand drifted to the hilt of her sword.

"What did you find out?" Caspian asked, his gaze intent on the disaster rushing their way.

"Enough," Maeve told him. "I know where we are going next, and I know we need to defeat the fae. The only outstanding question is how."

"How, indeed," Caspian replied.

And then the air was filled with the sound of footsteps.

23

HILL OF DRACONBANE

THE FINDER'S Stone pulsed against Maeve's chest, where she'd tucked it into her breastplate, squashed between her breasts. She could feel it, like a beast, breathing and pulsing, pointing her toward the dragon's lair. When she looked across the valley, she saw an opening in the mountains, a gaping hole leading down into darkness where she imagined tunnels twisted.

She flipped her sword in her hand as the goblins raced toward her and her companions, frustrated with the seemingly insurmountable obstacles they needed to push through to access the dragon's lair. The goblins were many and ferocious, but—she hoped—also inferior warriors, for the sea that raced toward them was massive and overwhelming. She turned toward Caspian and stuck out a hand. "It has been an honor," she told him.

He shook his head, although his cheek curved up in a hint of a smile. "Maeve, why would you say such a thing?"

"Don't you see what's rushing toward us?" She pointed into the valley, which was no longer peaceful or beautiful.

Caspian shrugged, a foolish grin on his handsome face as he drew his sword. "Maeve, they are only goblins. As I always say, believe in the best possible outcome. We can take them."

Maeve shook her head. How? "A warlord to the bitter end," she murmured, a fire rising in her belly.

"A warlord to the sweet end," Caspian disagreed, and then he began to run.

Maeve wanted to scream, demand for him to stop, but then the fire rose within her too, engulfing her with a desperate desire for blood. She wanted—needed—to fight, to slay, to kill them all. A battle cry left her lips and, taking her blade in both hands, she ran down the hill toward the horde of goblins.

The melee spread about her and she dived in, cleaving head from body, limb from limb, and striking down knives, axes, and swords as the goblins surged about her. It was like an unending sea rushing down into a waterfall—waves crashing against waves in an unstoppable force. Pinpricks of pain shot through her legs, arms, and core as short knives drove into her again and again. But she refused to stop and kept moving forward until she reached the middle of the valley, slinging bodies across it as the rage within her let loose and she fought to reach the lair.

For a long time, there was nothing but cries and screams, death throes of the goblins and she knew not what else. Although the sun was bright and high, she lost track of Caspian and had no idea where the pirates were. Even Sandrine was lost in the cacophony of sound. There was nothing but the killing. She wished she could bring this kind of violence down on the heads of the fae, but since they weren't there, the goblins would have to be a substitute. But it wasn't enough; it would never be enough. Each kill should have eased her conscience, but she still felt the darkness in her soul. Sobs rose in her throat as she fought. She whirled, twirled, slashed, and slayed, the rage pouring through her as she fought. Pointed ears went down and goblins shrieked in agony, but each one that fell was replaced with another. Maeve raced through the valley, down the slope of flattened grass, and up through the white blossoms where they gyrated in a sort of dance, celebrating a victory that never came.

Maeve's legs moved faster as the snarls of the goblins and the shouts of her companions echoed behind her. She sprinted up the hill, her breath coming thick and fast until she arrived at the entrance to the lair. The yawning mouth of the cavern stood open, and on either side of the opening were chiseled stones with runes carved into them, words of an old age marking the spot.

If the battle rage hadn't been running hot through her veins, she might have been frightened by the sheer immensity of the lair. Instead, she dashed inside, her screams echoing through the tunnels. Darkness invaded her vision, but the Finder's Stone pulsed, faster than before. Maeve twisted and turned, moving deeper into the lair until suddenly, she was there, at the foot of the hall of treasures.

Precious jewels captured her vision. More jewels than she'd ever seen in her life, a pit of gold—a pit of desire—running deep into the mountains. She stared at it, aghast, spinning as she took it all in. The treasure of Draconbane, the lair of dragons. Wealth beyond her wildest dreams glittered before her eyes. There was a humming in her ears, a low pulse, a beat, a well of uncontrolled lust.

A raw scream came loose from her throat and she dashed down, spraying gold coins, rubies, diamonds, and sapphires everywhere. The jewels sprawled around her, and she could do nothing but leave them there, glittering where they lay. She sank to her knees in the middle of the treasure, a searing pain in her chest. This was the treasure she had searched for; this was all she needed. All her years of hiring out her skills, fighting for others, when the wealth of the world was in Draconbane. A heat rose in her cheeks and for a moment, her thoughts drifted in a haze of greed. The thought entered her mind abruptly: here in the dragon's lair, away from the goblins, away from the fae, she was free. What if she ignored the fae and their demands? What if she took the treasure and sailed north, sailed far, so far away that they would never find her and could never use the collar on her again. Would it work if she ran?

Maeve was lost in her own thoughts until a roar pulled her back into reality. She stood up, shaking loose coins off her knees, suddenly disgusted at her weakness. How easily the treasure had overwhelmed her and made her forget what was real.

The cry came again, and this time she recognized it. It was partly distressed and partly frustrated, but she dared not ignore it, for it was the voice of someone she knew. Someone she loved. The sound broke through her thoughts like sunlight shattering fog. The past year she'd warred with her feelings, and although she was still unsure whether it was brotherly love or romantic love, it didn't matter. She needed to help him.

Maeve spun on her heel to head back to the tunnels, toward where the cry had come from. As she did, a gold sheen flickered on the edge of her vision. High above her was a gilded cage, and within it knelt what looked like a woman. In the quick glance, all Maeve saw was the woman bent over an object covered in blue dust. Without a doubt, Maeve knew she needed to ascend to that cliff and speak with that woman, but she couldn't leave her companion to fend for himself. She'd return once she helped Caspian.

Jewels shifted around her as she ran, heart thumping, back to the entrance of the dragon's lair, where the sides of the mountain narrowed down to a passageway that curved and twisted like the body of a snake. Maeve tore around a corner, ignoring the way her minor wounds wept and burned as dust clung to them.

As she rounded a second corner, she came up short, taking in the backside of an oversize goblin. A layer of dust covered its green skin, dulling it in the shadows of the lair, and it wore what was once a white cloth around its loins. Other than that, it was naked, with gangly arms and legs. It lifted a mace in one hand and swung it, eliciting another hoarse cry.

"Aye!" Maeve shouted, scooping up a rock and hurling it at the broad backside of the goblin.

It swung around, its wide, conniving eyes bulging from its flat head while its sharp nose poked out like a blade from its face. Its face was skeletal and misshappen, and its thin lips pulled back, displaying a row of razor-sharp teeth. As its nostrils twitched, a low snarl came from its throat, and then a tail snaked out, so fast Maeve could not leap away in time. It wrapped around her ankle and pulled, hurling her to the ground. The breath whooshed out of her and she almost dropped her sword as the surprisingly strong tail yanked her forward. Dust flew up like a cloud, obscuring the goblin from her vision. Maeve scrambled, managing to bring the sword down where she thought the tail was. There was a cry as the goblin let go and stepped back with a hiss.

Maeve sprung to her feet, allowing the battle rage to

take her. She lashed out with a cry, whipping her sword around to waist height, where she guessed the goblin would strike next. She was right, and her steel clanged against the mace the creature carried, but she was surprised at the strength with which the goblin pushed back. She whipped her sword away and slashed toward its heart, but the goblin was just as fast, anticipating her movements and striking hard again and again. Maeve screamed as she fought, a howl of rage gurgling up from within. She ignored the weariness in her arms, the shaking of her legs, the rawness of her throat, and the terror that gripped her heart. If Caspian was behind the goblin, mortally wounded, she had to kill it, save him, find Sandrine, and ask her—or rather, beg and demand at sword's edge—for her to heal him. The warlord had been her only friend through the last year, her best year, and she could not lose him now. Especially when it was her fault for asking for his assistance on her dangerous quest. With the goblin horde outside, and the monstrous gatekeeper—she didn't know how she'd missed the creature when she'd run inside—she finally understood the terror that the word Draconbane invoked in peoples' hearts.

The goblin shrieked as it fought, its putrid breath coming toward her. The air was sour and stank like rotten eggs. Sweat beaded on Maeve's forehead and she kicked, her foot smacking into the beast's loincloth. It paused and shuddered, and that shudder was just enough. Using both hands and cursing her lack of strength, she lifted her blade and sliced through the goblin's neck. There was one mournful moment where it swayed in place, its eyes bugging out of its head. And then the head fell back and a spurt of blood shot up toward the walls of the lair. Maeve sidestepped just in time as the goblin fell forward, right where she had been standing a moment before.

Wasting no time, she ran to the figure slumped on the ground behind the goblin.

"Caspian," she rasped.

Tears filled her eyes, blurring his face. He sat against the wall, where he must have dragged himself after she'd appeared to fight the goblin. There was blood all over his clothing, and he pressed his hand to a wound in his side. His mouth was bloody, his eyes cloudy, and yet one hand still held his sword, as though it were the only thing keeping him alive. Maeve knew it was likely because his fingers were wrapped so tightly around his sword that he could not have let it go if he'd wanted to. His blond hair was plastered to his head, which he turned slowly, eyes taking in Maeve and then shifting over to the goblin, as if he wasn't quite cognizant of what had happened. "Maeve," he whispered.

"Caspian." She bit back a cry and pressed her hand over his.

He winced in pain.

"Don't speak, don't talk, I'll find Sandrine and she'll heal you. You'll be fine."

"No," he gasped, trying to catch her eye. "Maeve.

Look at me. It's over. It's a mortal wound." He paused, panting between words as though he could not get in enough air to speak. "My time has come. I've been forgiven. I know what the Divine wishes of me. Maeve. My bag." His eyes dropped to his pack. "It's in there. It's yours."

Maeve shook her head. "Caspian." She reached up to cup his cheek. It was warm, rough, and a tear slid from her eye. "Don't say such things. What will I do without you?"

"Go on. You are brave. Strong. Beat them. Finish this. It's in my bag. I found it." He stopped abruptly, his eyes clearing and widening for a moment. Then his hand went slack, his head fell forward, and his eyes closed.

"No," Maeve whispered, "no, no. Please, no. Caspian. Don't leave me here, not like this," her body shook and, despite the danger, the dark, the stink of the place, and the quest that waited for her, she gathered him in her arms and sobbed.

She wasn't sure how much time had passed when she finally let go, her throat sore and eyes red and puffy. A hollowness centered in her core, and numbly, she reached for Caspian's bag, pulled it off him, and folded his hands over his chest. It seemed disrespectful to leave him there, in the hall next to the broken body of the oversize goblin. Already it was beginning to stink. The mace lay a few feet away, where it had fallen.

Tears still streaming down her cheeks, Maeve stared down at Caspian again. She longed to give him a proper burial, a warrior's burial, but to do that she needed a slab of stone, an arrow, and fire. Her thoughts flickered back to the inner lair, to the jewels flickering in the light. There was light there. If she moved quickly, she might be able to find a torch and return to give Caspian a proper burial.

Pain tore at her legs and arms as she rose, and when she looked down, crisscrossed patterns covered her legs where they had been sliced again and again with thin blades. Her vision went fuzzy, and she knew she needed something, food or water, before she continued. She opened Caspian's bag and pulled out the waterskin, tilting it back and emptying the contents into her mouth. The liquid was warm, but she did not care; it went down smoothly, dulling the pain in her throat. Her heavy breathing calmed, and she tossed the empty waterskin away. Tears, again, pricked at the corners of her eyes.

He looked so small and lonely slumped against the wall. As she surveyed the area, she realized she was alone. The goblins hadn't returned to defend their lair. Why was that? And where were Sandrine and the pirates? She'd seen them fighting, she was sure of it. But why would they leave her alone, unless . . . unless they were dead too? They had all been overrun by goblins.

Was it possible that she must continue on with her forced quest alone?

The thought jarred her, and she realized having companions had eased her burden. Who would she talk to? And who would believe that the fae were a threat, and she needed to stop them? If it even was possible to stop them. Her fingers clenched into fists. The odds were stacked against her and the one man she had counted on to assist her lay dead at her feet. Even Imer's words regarding Carn were insignificant. She was alone.

Her hand went limp inside Caspian's bag and her fingers touched something hard and long, like the stone that pulsed around her neck. She swallowed hard as she pulled it out. It was wrapped in cloth that fell open in her hands. Astonishment shot through her like an arrow, and she felt everything she thought she'd known falling, tearing, ripping apart. Her gaze went to Caspian, and she wanted to scream, wake him up, demand answers. How? When? Why?

The blue light shone off her face, revealing another shard, larger than the one she'd found in Lord Sebastian's fortress. Did Caspian mean the shard was hers? If so, when did he find it? Was this why he had been intent on coming with her? Did he have plans she knew nothing about?

She looked up and howled in frustration.

24

DRAGON'S LAIR

MAEVE WALKED BLINDLY down the passageway toward the lair where she'd seen the woman, if her eyes hadn't deceived her. She walked without purpose, a sheen of anger dancing on the edges of her vision. Her eyes clouded over again and again and there was a weight over her heart. A dread. An acknowledgement that something beyond her control was happening. Many things needed to be explained, and before she took another step toward helping her enemies and gaining her freedom, she needed answers. Answers she would choke out of the scholar on the edge of a knife if she could find the woman again. If Sandrine had been forthcoming, Caspian might not be dead. Yet the shard she'd taken from his bag threw her into confusion. He was part of this, fated, it seemed, but she did not understand why or how. Her memory returned to the night they'd spent in the Bawdy Sailor. He'd taken her shard, studied it, but why? What had he been looking for? What did he want with it?

A nasty thought crawled through her mind. For a year, she'd warred and served with Caspian. One year. But things changed. He went away for a time, claiming to visit a temple and study with a priest. When he came back, his goals were lofty, and he spoke incessantly about the Divine and becoming noble. He had still focused on finding treasure and making them wealthy, but he had also focused on other causes. For example, breaking up a slave trade, a mission that got her captured by the fae. Was that on purpose?

Her breath constricted in her throat and she reached out a hand, feeling the warm dust of the slick, smooth wall. Was Caspian working for the fae? Had he been captured by them and asked to find the lost relics? And then they decided he needed help and involved her? No. It couldn't be. She shouldn't think such things. It was terrible to think ill of the dead, and yet . . .

Or perhaps it wasn't what she thought, and only what the fae wished for her to think. What if they had chosen her because of her proximity to Caspian, one who already held a shard? But if they knew he had it, why did he still have it? Why let him keep it when they could have easily overpowered him? Unless they were playing some sick game with her, and the quest was more about her and less about the shards. And yet, the relic she was seeking had the power to break all curses. Not something to be taken lightly.

The pounding in her head increased until she pushed away the maddening thoughts. Thinking of such dark things would only drive her to the brink of sanity. Feeling hollow, she put one foot in front of the other until she reached the entrance to the lair, where jewels sparkled and light beamed, casting shadows upon the walls and conjuring magic tricks, making the area seem larger than it truly was, more threatening, shining with a deadly brilliance and encouraging trespassers to their deaths.

Maeve sensed the warning that hung in the air, the aura of doom, of blood. Was the treasure cursed? There was no way of knowing, and yet she feared so. The Finder's Stone pulsed against her chest, and suddenly her feet felt as heavy as the roots of the mountains. Much had happened in one single day. How could she find the willpower, the strength, to go on, when the things she valued, the people she cared about, were lost and tarnished?

Rather than giving in to another bout of tears, she lifted her head up and tried to find what she'd seen out of the corner of her eye earlier. The glimmer of blue caught her attention, and when she turned in the glow's direction, she saw, once again, the cage. It had gold bars and a domed top, large enough for a small person to stand up straight in, even though the woman inside knelt. Stringy hair hung down around her face, making it difficult to tell whether she was asleep or praying.

Maeve flashed back to her imprisonment in the dungeon of the damned and how she'd felt in her prison cell, waiting, biding her time until the right opportunity came along. Who was this woman and why was she locked up? Was she a prisoner of the goblins? Maeve shuddered at the thought, unwilling to imagine what kinds of horrors the woman may have been subject to during her captivity.

The light flickered, sending shadows dancing. Shapes of dark monsters rose from the walls and faded again, as though the light was sending her a warning. In that transition, Maeve saw stairs pressed up against the walls, leading toward the cage. And then she saw there was more than one flight of stairs and more than one cage. Most of them were empty, but she thought she saw stark white bones in one, and revulsion swept through her.

Caspian's death drifted to the back of her mind and she moved toward the stairs. A vast array of jewels lay in her path, forcing her to step on them, her feet sinking down slightly as the jewels crunched under her weight. When she first saw them, she'd thought of taking them, but now as she walked over the hoard, she realized it was all blood money. Treasure that belonged to the last remnant of a lost race. Who knew what atrocious acts had been done to collect such wealth? Perhaps those sins, those crimes, were the reason all the dragons were gone, and nothing but a murderous horde of goblins dwelled in the mountains.

Even as Maeve thought it, she saw a reflection in herself. The things she'd done in the past she'd weighed only against herself and her motives, but thieving and killing in exchange for wealth was wrong, wasn't it? Who knew how many untold hundreds had been damaged by her actions? She'd never thought of them; she'd only fought to complete her contract and get paid.

The weight of her guilt struck her again. This predicament was her own fault; she wasn't one of the innocents who had done nothing to deserve her fate. The fae had said as much when they captured her; they could only do so because of the darkness in her heart. That was why Caspian had changed. He'd seen the darkness in his heart and started embarking on quests that benefitted others to try and complete a few acts that would show the Divine his change of heart. But had that change of heart ultimately led to his death? Would he have been better off staying a shallow, simple warlord? It was maddening not knowing.

The stairs were rough, crudely hacked into the mountainside, but clear of jewels. Maeve ascended quickly, determined to keep her feet moving, for if she slowed down, exhaustion would catch up with her and she did not know if she could move another muscle once that happened. The strenuous climb made her cuts reopen, and every now and then she felt blood trickle down her legs. By the time she reached the top, her legs were burning, but in front of her was the golden cage.

She attempted to catch her breath as she approached, eyeing the woman. Her chest moved in and out, signaling that she still drew breath, her filthy fingers were clasped in her lap, as though she were praying, and a threadbare cloak was laid under her bare knees. She wore a kind of short skirt that must have fallen mid-thigh when she stood upright, and a thin, sleeveless shift covered her body. It was so worn there were holes in places, showing skin covered with a layer of dirt.

Maeve took another step, swallowing hard. A blue item did indeed lie in front of the woman's knees. It was another shard, this one as big as Maeve's forearm and pulsing with an inner light. Her eyes were drawn to it and riveted there. It was beautiful.

She took a breath, unsure. The shards were holy relics—she had no right to touch them. What the fae were making her do was wrong. The crown should be left in pieces, and yet she wanted to reach out and take the shard for herself, put them all back together, and see what the crown looked like. Perhaps even wear it. Blood rushed through her ears, and then a pulsing came, a warning hum, and she faltered, taking a step back as fear gripped her. Such thoughts of greed had never entered her mind before; they were dark, unnatural, and although she was supposed to be a queen, taking a holy relic for herself was not right. If the Divine had seen fit to destroy it, it shouldn't be put back together.

Awareness of who she was, or should be, roared through her ears. Queen of nothing. Survivor of Carn. But none of that meant anything at all; not her supernatural strength, not her ability to fight and win—nothing mattered. All she felt was the crushing weight of guilt and sorrow. This was wrong. All wrong. Everything she'd done thus far had led up to this moment, a reaction to her actions. Blame the circumstance as much as she might, she realized it all came down to choice. She'd always had a choice, and she'd always chosen to go the corrupt route, to destroy life, to give in to her selfish desires and do nothing else. Everything she'd done in her life was self-serving, which is why she deserved what was happening to her now, happening not only to herself, but also to the world.

"It's not your fault."

Maeve's head jerked up and her mouth came open, the cry of astonishment dying in her throat. The woman had opened her eyes; they were reptilian, golden and lidded, giving her face an eerie look when she blinked. Her gaze was direct, penetrating, without mercy, and other than raising her head, she had not moved.

25

GOBLIN QUEEN

"Did you speak?" Maeve whispered, the power in the air stealing her breath away.

"I know why you are here," the woman went on, as though she hadn't heard Maeve's question. "My time is over. The night of the fae falls nigh. Kingdoms rise and fall, all in time, but it must be the right time, deemed so by fate."

Maeve shook her head in confusion. Was this woman mad?

"Not mad," the woman said, "but I have languished in captivity for too long. According to the Prophecy of Erinyes: '*A day will come when curses will be broken, the lost shall be found, the found shall be lost, and the rift between mortal and celestial will cease to exist.*' That day is coming and you can do nothing to stop it, only circumvent its finality."

Maeve stiffened. She found it disconcerting that the woman seemed able to read her mind. She shifted from foot to foot, trying to ignore the way her legs ached and burned. A drop of blood ran down her shin and weariness chipped away at her spirit.

"I have come for the shard," she said. "That is all."

The lips of the woman rose as though in a smile, but there was no smile on her thin cheeks, nor in her reptilian eyes. Reaching out, she picked up the shard in both hands and ran her fingers over it, stroking it lovingly, as though she wished never to be parted from it. "Listen, Maeve of Carn, and listen well. If you want the shard, you need to hear me out and understand what is beyond your control. Isn't that what you seek? What you desire? Knowledge, above all?"

Her tone was gentle, intoxicating, and wormed its way through Maeve's mind. Questions flittered away, and she found herself sitting down and crossing her legs, but not of her own accord. What magic did this woman have? What power over her? She desperately wanted to hear and understand, at last, the knowledge that had been kept from her. Did she have time before the goblins returned and hemmed her in with their sharp teeth, wicked knives, and nasty blows?

"If you want to understand what is coming, you will listen to me." The women spoke steadily, but her fingers never stopped stroking the shard. "My name is Ariefluer of Draconbane, and I am its last mage. My power lies in the mind, in reading auras and sensing thoughts. If your mind is open, I can read it, not that I need to, for I can guess at what you might think. People are not as complex as they think they are, and it's simple to unravel them once I've discovered what they desire. Your desire drives you; it's plain on your face. You want knowledge, you're tired of being controlled, and I sense a darkness within you, a desire for revenge that's deep and driving. Guilt weighs you down, but you should not dwell on it. There is no hope for me now, but there is for you. This is why you are here, why I've sat here, waiting for someone like you. It makes sense, now that I see you. The fae took you, threatened you, and collared you. But in seeking what they do, they will bring about their own ruin. Draconbane was conquered by the fae, long ago. They killed the last dragons, imprisoned me with a dark curse, and took my sister."

Sister. Some of the tension in Maeve's body eased. But Draconbane was conquered five hundred years ago; how was this woman alive now? Was her sister still alive?

Those golden eyes bored into her. "My sister is not what you would think. Unlike me, she is not gifted with magic of the mind, but we have one similarity. We are both powerful beyond measure when we are in our true forms, our second skin, but when the fae cursed me, they made a mistake. There was a weakness in their spell that allowed me to turn the curse on the fae themselves. If I cannot walk in the daylight, they cannot either, aside from the night of the full moon each month.

If I am cursed, so are the fae, and so is my sister. Nothing can break our curse except for the Seven Shards of Erinyes."

Fear rippled through Maeve. A second skin? What was it? Were the sisters dangerous? Evil? There must have been at least a thread of darkness within them that brought the fae to them.

"My curse is to live my days out here, in this cave, without my power, but I've had years to think on my plight. Once I give you the shard, I will turn into dust, and once again my soul shall sing. I'll be free to fly."

"Why are you telling me this?" Maeve demanded.

The reptilian eyes blinked, a double lid coming over them, creating a film and then disappearing.

Maeve shivered under the glare of the woman.

"I tell you this because of my sister. Watch out for her. We were both wicked in our own ways, one just as bad as the other, but there's a reason the fae left me here and took her as a bride. Yet, I don't believe she was captured unwillingly—I think she wanted the fae, desired the king of the fae for some reason. Perhaps there is more to the story than even I know. That is for you to find out. But be warned: my sister stopped at nothing to get rid of me. I don't know what she would do to others who stand in her way. Perhaps she is aligned with the fae, or perhaps she is using them."

Maeve folded her hands in her lap, linking them together to hold on to some sort of reasoning, some stability. If what the woman told her was true, she was in deeper trouble than she'd ever considered. "Why the quest for the seven shards, then? Why send me here, when all they needed to do was open up a portal and take what you have kept all these years? How did they not know?"

This time the woman did smile, a cruel, haunting smile that revealed a row of sharp incisors. Her mouth was full of fangs, and for a moment Maeve thought her heart would stop. Was she talking to a demon? A fae? Was that the second skin the woman spoke of?

"My sister did not attend to her studies. She was intent on physical manifestations, so much so she forgot about the mind being a powerful tool. My ability to manipulate the mind made me great. I knew about the Seven Shards of Erinyes because I studied. I found this shard buried in the treasury and swallowed it whole before the fae came. I birthed it out like a child and took care of it while I waited, knowing that one day my sister would find out and send someone to retrieve it. And I knew she had to send someone, because the fae cannot open portals into Draconbane. There are grounds where it is impossible for them to work their dark magic, which is why they need you."

Maeve held on to those words. Places where it would be impossible for the fae to reach her? Did the scholar know about these places and withheld that information? "Where else? What other areas are off-limits to the fae?"

The woman's smile faded, and she shrugged. "I

know not. My sights were set on protecting my realm and interfering with the celestials; that knowledge you must gain from others."

Ideas were already forming in Maeve's mind. If the fae could not reach her here during the night of the full moon, she could hide and wait them out. The collar around her neck hummed, as though the fae could listen to her treacherous thoughts. "Do you have books?" she asked, breathless. "Old scrolls? Anything that I might read?"

The woman blinked slowly, her eyes drifting down to the shard, and then she thrust it toward Maeve. "Draconbane contains a wealth of knowledge. There are books, scrolls, and endless treasures here, but they are impossible to take because of my guard. From the looks of you, you fought through my guard on your way in."

"Guard?" Maeve faltered, although her fingers stretched out toward the shard.

"Goblins." The woman continued to hold the end of the shard, her odd eyes boring into Maeve. "I've done you a boon and saved this shard for you, and now it's time for one last favor."

"Favor?" Maeve faltered. The woman was in no shape to offer favors.

"Aye. The goblin horde worships me as their queen. As they should. I'm the only queen they've ever known. When I die, they will disintegrate into chaos as they hunt for another queen. I will give you my stone. It will not be effective long after I die, but as long as the link lasts and you carry it, the goblins will not harm you. Once my ashes are cool, the link will break and they will come after you, so if you want to live, you will go far away from here before that time comes."

Frustration ripped through Maeve, and she all but snatched the shard away from the mage's hands. "Why should I trust you?"

The woman shrugged, her thin shoulders moving up and down underneath her filthy gown. "I have told you many things; they could be false tales to mislead you, or they could be true. In the end, you will have to trust your heart, trust yourself. It is not up to me to decide who you should or shouldn't trust. Words carry no weight if the actions behind them are meaningless. Take this." She reached behind her, then held out a round object.

It was oval and large, like a melon. The color was off-white, and yet it glistened in the light. It looked like an egg. Maeve stared at it, eyes wide. If she had to guess, she'd say it was a dragon egg, cursed by the mage perhaps? A symbol of her power?

"Take it," the mage encouraged, although it was too big to fit between the golden bars of the cage. "Seeing is believing, isn't it? The rest you will need faith for. Faith. Something I've never been so fortunate to have."

Maeve hesitated, an idea coming to her. "I will take it, and protect what is inside if I can, but only if you tell me how to defeat the fae."

The woman shook her head. "You are a bold one,

aren't you? But alas, there is no room for you to bargain. What is done is done. If you would defeat the fae, you must find your own way. If you recall, my kingdom fell to their rule, the greatest kingdom in those days, and if something so great can fall, what chance do you stand against them?"

A cry of rage burst from Maeve's throat.

The mage eyed her, considering. "You are desperate, aren't you? I sense the same feeling I had, years ago, when the fae invaded my mountains. When my sister turned against me. I would have done anything to survive, anything to stop them and go back to those days of glory. But I also recognized my thoughts had turned dark, and that I had aligned myself with evil people. I heard whispers, though one would need to speak to a scholar to confirm them."

Maeve's chest tightened. A scholar? The term was used widely, but her immediate thoughts flew to Sandrine, and a dark awakening stirred in her belly.

"A scholar to confirm what?"

"To confirm how to eternally banish the fae to the shadow world."

"But isn't that where they are now? Cursed? And if curses can be broken, what is the point of confining them to the shadow world?"

"Ah. That you will have to discover for yourself. Like I said before, my quest to destroy the fae ended in bloodshed and sorrow. I've heard word that one must go north. I've also heard that one must go to the western islands. It is a quest you will need to take up on your own. My advice is, know your enemy. Discover their weakness and use that to bring them down. And above all, stay patient. Revenge is not for the faint of heart. Now. I've said enough, and my strength is waning. Hurry. Before the goblins return."

The woman sat the egg down and pushed it toward the golden bars. She took a deep breath, arched her back, and spread out her arms. Her lips moved soundlessly, reciting a spell, or perhaps a prayer.

Maeve held up her hands. "Please, wait. There is more that you know, isn't there? I still have questions. What about your sister? Does she still dwell with the fae? You said she did not study the world, but to know what she knows, would she use a scholar? Please!"

The woman ignored her and a smell like an iron forge burning filled the air. A mist grew in the cage and swirled around the woman, momentarily hiding her from sight. Then, before Maeve's eyes, her body turned to dust and whisked away in the air.

Maeve gasped and stumbled backward. For a moment, she thought she saw wings, massive and leathery with hooked claws on the edges, and then there was nothing. The cage disappeared, leaving only a mound of dust with the egg sitting in the center. Free at last.

Sounds echoed through the silence: the clacking of feet and the licking of tongues. Maeve straightened and took a step toward the egg, even as her vision swam.

She wanted to scream, curse, beg, and plead. The woman had given her hope, and yet the hope invoked more fear than she'd ever felt. It was as though she was in the grips of something unknown with the strength of a waterfall, yanking her downstream to the mouth of terror and there was nothing she could do.

Tears poured down her cheeks as she reached for the egg. Its heat surprised her and she almost dropped it, crying out at the instant pain that ripped through her fingers. She scanned the area, surprised to see that the ragged cloak had somehow survived the transformation of the mage. She used it to pick up the egg and turned toward the stairs. Caspian. She had to give him a warrior's salute before the goblins returned.

26

BEYOND THE VALLEY

TEARS STREAMED DOWN Maeve's face as she buried Caspian. She'd taken him to the treasure room and laid him in an alcove after sweeping out the mound of treasure. When the time came to cremate his remains, her heart stopped her. She just couldn't. Besides, his face looked so peaceful lying there. The creases were gone from around his eyes, his lips had relaxed, and it looked as though a sweet dream filled his thoughts. Silent tears rolled down her cheeks and dripped off her chin. Without bothering to wipe them away, she folded Caspian's cool hands on his chest.

"Caspian," she promised, "dear Caspian. I don't know what happened nor why you carried one of the lost shards, but I promise to find a way to stop the fae from taking and destroying. I will make you proud and discover what it means to be noble."

She lifted her chin as the words left her mouth and her blue eyes flashed in defiance. She would do this for Caspian, and nothing would stand in her way.

Taking the bundle of rags in one hand, she stood tall. Time was short and the stomping of feet warned her the goblins would reach the treasure room soon. Would the woman's claim about the egg ring true? Part of her wanted to curse, rage, and wail, especially at the loss of all the knowledge the mage had collected. But there was nothing for it. Even if she could find a place to hide until the night of the full moon, she'd have to deal with the goblins eventually.

Stepping out into the passageway, she began to run. The bloodthirsty cries of the tireless creatures chased her. Yet as the cries rang on, Maeve recognized a sorrow in them, a deep and mournful note, as if they knew the prisoner they kept in a gilded cage had flown, escaped, and there was no queen to worship anymore.

A flash of green reared up in front of her and the reek of unwashed bodies assaulted her nose. Maeve took long strides and held her sword in one hand. A recklessness washed over her, tugging her to let go of her restraint and run into the multitude of goblins to see what they would do.

A high shriek pierced her eardrums when they saw her. They surged toward her, like the current of a mighty river. Battle rage boiled in Maeve's belly and her eyes sparked with hate. She lifted her sword, ready to give in to her emotions, to demand blood for blood. But as she reached the first segment of goblins, they sprang away, shrieking. Maeve halted, heart hammering in her throat. She took a step. The goblins scattered, as though her aura were holy and they were not allowed to approach. She took another step, and another, growing bold as the goblins scattered away, some hissing, others bowing, but none daring to approach her. Slowly, she slid her sword back into her scabbard and held the egg in front of her with two hands, lifting it high as she strode boldly out of the lair.

The low light of the dying sun made her blink hard. As she descended into the valley, she saw dead goblins lining the slope. There were charred remains on their clothing and some of them were still smoking. She sniffed. Aside from blood, there was a charred scent in the air, and a dark smoke so intense it made her nose itch. What was this? Who had done this? She hadn't recalled the smell of fire before as she fought her way to the lair, but then she'd been enthralled in her battle rage, which led her to forget about anything and everything else.

She scanned the hillside, wondering where Sandrine and the pirates were, if they had made it through alive. Come to think of it, they hadn't followed her and Caspian into the lair—of that she was sure. It was like the first shard; Sandrine had chosen to stay out of sight while Maeve faced trouble alone. A sudden bitterness rose through her, tasting sour on her tongue, though perhaps that was the bile in the back of her throat.

Her legs ached as she climbed the hill and exhaustion set in. She hadn't realized how hard she'd fought and how emotionally spent she was. The words of the woman echoed in her mind, and while she wanted to make sense of it, she also needed to get as far away from Draconbane as possible. Although it was the only true safe haven from the fae she knew of, it could only be a last resort.

"Maeve."

The hushed whisper of her name, nothing more than a question in the wind, made her open her eyes. She hadn't realized they were closed until she opened them and looked up. On the crest of the hill stood Imer, his clothes ripped, his fashionable hat gone, and his boots covered in a slick substance that might have been a combination of blood and guts. It looked as though his clothes were burned, and his face was covered in soot, like he'd been through a fire, though the skin showing through his clothing was hairy and unblemished by flame.

Maeve stared at him, unsure what she should say or even do. "Where are they?" she croaked out.

There was a haunted look in his dark eyes as he dropped his gaze and ran his fingers through his dirty, slicked-back hair. "Is Caspian . . ."

A bolt of rage flashed through Maeve, instant and

shocking, like a flash of lightning. "Don't you dare speak ill of the dead," she snarled. Just as quickly as it came, her anger faded, leaving a hollowness so gaping she thought she'd fall into it and never find herself again.

"Come," he held out a hand, his fingertips stained with ash. "You've fought hard enough. Come, rest."

His face blurred in her vision as tears swam in her eyes. She forced her unwilling legs to the top of the hill, even though they felt like lead. Imer's hand closed around her arm, so warm it was almost hot to her skin. But his touch was comforting, and she leaned into it, willing to give up the struggle, give in, rest, and let her mind drift.

As Caspian always said, problems were best solved when given a night of sleep, for sleep was healing, and when refreshed and in full health, solutions were always found.

Caspian. He had been a positive influence in her life; solid, steady—a home. What would she do without him?

Maeve vaguely remembered being led to an enclosure between the mountains, where a stream flowed through the stones, creating a pool shaded by fir trees. Imer helped her wash the blood off her legs, refilled her waterskin, and told her to rest as he tucked her underneath a tree branch and she snuggled up against a brown trunk with moss as a cushion for her head.

When she woke, hours later, a sliver of the almost-full moon hung in the sky, lighting up the shadows with hues of silver. She glimpsed a hint of beauty in the twinkle in the starlight, the magic in the moonlight, and the way the pool glittered underneath it all. It was as if the pool allowed the moon to shine its face upon the surface of its water and worship the lake.

Maeve propped herself up on one elbow, and as she did, the egg rolled away. She'd slept with it tucked against her stomach, and the sight of it brought back the memories of the day. The magic in the moonlight faded and the loss of Caspian threatened to flatten her. She scooped the egg up and sat cross-legged with it in her lap. Leaning back against the tree, she closed her eyes and recalled the conversation she'd had with the mage. Even though the goblins had overrun the lair, a spark of hope lit up in her. Perhaps there was a way to hide the shards from the fae. If they could not enter certain places, she needed to find one of those places and hide. If she were hidden—with the shards—they could not find them. And then it struck her like a blow to the chest.

The fae did not know about the shard Caspian carried. As long as she kept it hidden, apart from the others, she could keep them from completing the crown, keep them from taking over the world. Hope surged within her. It would not all be for naught. She would find a way.

Satisfied with a solution to her dilemma, she

squinted in the moonlight, searching for Imer, Ingram, and Sandrine. She did not recall seeing them earlier, but the pool was quiet and the surrounding area dense and wooded. Perhaps she was alone, left to herself after securing the shard, but something about that did not make sense.

Sandrine wanted the shards, and surely she would have appeared after the battle, crudely reminding Maeve it was time to continue to the next location. Sandrine the scholar, whose book Maeve intended to steal. The need had become more urgent, dire even. Sandrine's book might contain the location of places where the fae could not open portals. She needed to find one as soon as she was able. As long as she kept Caspian's shard separate, when the fae came for the others, she could hand them over, and they would suspect nothing.

At the thought, the heat of the collar did not flare up, nor did the faint echo of the Master's words. She'd discovered a way to combat them, and while she did not want to hide for the rest of her life, she would do what she had to do to save the world. Even Caspian would consider it a noble act.

In remembrance of him, she rocked onto her knees and folded her hands in front of her. It had been weeks since she whispered prayers to the Divine, and yet on such a moonlit night it felt right. She closed her eyes, lips moving in a murmured prayer. A peace overwhelmed her, closing around her, softening her sorrow and reminding her she had a purpose, a place. It was all right. Everything would work out as the Divine intended.

Relaxing, Maeve lay back down against the tree trunk and returned to her slumber.

27

WIZARD'S SANCTUM

HUSHED WHISPERS BROKE the silence of the inner sanctum, and Jacq the wizard stood up straight, letting his heavy robes hang off his shoulders. He lifted his hands, palms upright, and closed his eyes, listening to the voice of the winds. Some days, the whispers of the wind were easy to decipher, but others, it was blurred, like reading the future while looking through a marred mirror. He sensed the strange cadence in the voices, the sign that something had changed, something had happened. But what? He needed knowledge, information . . .

"Jacq."

A feminine voice interrupted his meditation, and he opened his eyes, purposefully keeping his feelings from displaying on his face. "Willow," he said, studying his apprentice, who stood in the doorway.

She was striking, with the shades of her dark skin

offset by the long-sleeved, form-fitting red dress she wore. Its silk skirts, laced at the end, swept the stone floor as she moved. Her black hair was unbound and flowed in a collection of waves and curls down to her waist. As always, she looked beautiful, wild, intoxicating, and dangerous.

When she first arrived at his hidden village, Imperia, more commonly called the wizard's tower, he'd recognized their kindred spirits. At first, he tried to keep her at a distance, but quickly realized her power called out to his, and that he could not hide from a powerful mage like Willow. Instead, he began to teach her. Mages came and went, but it was Willow who stayed by his side. He saw her as his successor, but he was aware she saw herself as more, so much more than a mere keeper of power, instructor of mages, and next in line to guide Imperia.

She stepped into the room. The sanctum was a circular structure at the summit of the tower with walls made of high windows that ran from the floor to the ceiling. A cascade of golden light made the room shimmer, and often it seemed as though Jacq could see the power around him manifesting as words and visions dancing in the daylight. The stone floor was covered in runes and patterns that only added to the enchantment. The sanctum was where Jacq came to meditate and listen to the whispers the wind carried to his ears. Whispers of change and disruptions in the land.

"Forgive my intrusion, but Kel has returned,"

Willow said. She did not look sorry at all for interrupting him, and a slight smile played around her lips.

Jacq folded his hands together. Kel was Willow's white hawk, with which she shared a magical bond. When asked, she'd send the bird out to fly across the land, bringing back news of what it saw. The connection between Willow and Kel was potent, unusual. Jacq had never heard of a mage who could send power into a creature without turning it into a monster.

"Proceed," Jacq encouraged her.

"Ingram and Imer are in the Draconbane Mountains, with three others."

Three? That was unusual. He had only expected two others to join them. "Are they being followed?"

Willow shook her head and pursed her lips. "Not yet."

Relief surged through Jacq. "Good. Our diversion was successful and the quest still stands."

"But the night of the full moon is near . . ." Willow trailed off. She moved closer to Jacq and lifted her eyes to the doomed ceiling. Light danced across her face and bare throat as she breathed in. "I sense a change. . ."

Finally. Willow had never read the winds before, nor sensed a change. If she could feel it now, it meant either her power was growing stronger or what had happened was so strong it impacted the elements. But what was it? That he could not gain a sense of, but perhaps she could. "Still your mind," he coached her. "Listen to the whispers of the wind. What does it tell you?"

Willow listened, head thrown back, taking slow, shaky breaths.

Jacq watched the smooth skin of her neck throb as she swallowed, and then her eyes met his, dark and intense. "Do you remember?" she whispered, as though not to disturb the whispering voices in the sanctum. "When you first taught me of power and helped me understand the rush of emotions that twist through me? You told me the power of a mage is always strongest when united with others. You also told me about the Prophecy of Erinyes. When it comes true, we will be seen not as corrupt souls with powers that should be controlled, but the saviors of the land." Her eyes changed, widening in awareness. "But you never told me you were cursed, bound to this tower, which is why you need others to do your bidding for you. When the prophecy comes true, you will be free too."

He nodded in encouragement, afraid to break the spell of knowledge with his words. His heart beat faster, hoping she would go on. Was his prodigy becoming stronger than him?

"But you aren't like the cursed ones." Her hands reached out, catching his own and holding tight. "Because you don't want to rule the world—you want to change it. The prophecy mentions 'the lost' who shall be found, but there's more to it, isn't there?"

He looked down at their joined hands, and a hum of power cut through the whispers in the wind. "Aye, there is more to the prophecy. A day will come when curses will be broken. The lost shall be found, the found shall be lost, and the rift between mortal and celestial will cease to exist. The dragon queen of old will rise, freed but hidden in disguise. The last defender will come forth, and the sword of justice will purify."

The hum grew louder as they held hands, locked in a rush of power that whirled around them like a windstorm. Jacq studied her eyes, watching as they grew wider and as more and more power shimmered behind them. She felt what he felt, their union, strengthened as they held hands until it became overwhelming. With a cry, Willow let go and spun away, breathing hard.

When she regained her breath, she said, "When our hands were joined, I heard the whispers in the wind clearly. A queen of old was freed from a curse using the power of death, yet her spirit lives on. The last defender has been found, but has not come forth." She turned back to Jacq, her eyes imploring as she took one shuddering breath after the other, like one recovering from the heights of pleasure. "I thirst for knowledge, like you do. I can see your mind, your thoughts, your desires. But I don't know why. Not yet. Tell me more, teach me, so that we shall be ready when the curses are broken."

Jacq caught her hand in his and pulled her back toward him, his mind churning with her words. A queen of old freed. Ingram and Imer in Draconbane. The last defender found. They were close. So close. "Willow, stay with me for a bit longer, and I will share with you all I know. Listen to the wind. The night of the full moon is near. We need to know about the shards and the sword."

"We need to prepare for war, we need alliances and armies, but we are the hunted," Willow puzzled. "How can we fight when there are so few of us?"

Jacq wrapped his arms around her, relishing the power that twisted around them when they touched. "In days of old, the mages fought together, and so we will strategize together and find a way. But first, we need to know more. I have done research, but it is not enough. We must be prepared when the shards are restored into a crown, and all curses are broken."

28

FOREST OF PINE AND FIR

When morning dawned, they were all there. Imer was wearing his hat again, and he'd washed the soot off his face, although his clothes still hung in shreds, showing off glimpses of his lean, hard body. Maeve could not deny the gravitational pull, the slight attraction toward him, and yet her sorrow masked all other feelings. Questions rose on her tongue when she saw Sandrine, bent over, looking grayer and more tired than she'd ever appeared. Yet her chin was lifted, and she carried the book in her hands, arms wrapped around it as though she could protect it from the elements. Ingram lagged and there was a slight limp to his step. What had they done out here in the valley? Clearly, they'd fought to save her from something, but what? Did she dare ask? In spite of her curiosity, Maeve held her tongue, knowing she carried secrets of her own that would not be pried from her lips. Sandrine gave her nothing but a brief nod. "Do you have it, girl?" she asked, her voice hoarse and rough.

Maeve nodded once.

Sandrine pressed her lips together and took the lead, weaving past the pool and heading directly south. Maeve followed while Imer and Ingram moved to the back. There were no questions asked about Caspian, and Maeve assumed Imer had told them. She swallowed a sob, burying her feelings with dogged determination. She would see this through and make him proud. If his spirit rested above with the celestials, perhaps he would look down upon her, follow her progress, and know his sacrifice was for the greater good.

They trudged through the forest of pine and fir trees in silence, each lost in their own thoughts. The path they followed was wide open, leaving room for three to travel abreast. It twisted and turned, leading them to the crest of hilltops only to dive back down into deep valleys. All the while, the evergreen trees hid the view from them, and hid them from any hostile creatures they might encounter. The pace was slow, strenuous, and often they paused, allowing Sandrine a moment to huff and puff, and then carry on as though it did not matter. Maeve glanced at her now and again, wondering how strong the woman was. Her determination was boundless, but would her body fail her?

It wasn't until late afternoon that Maeve gave voice

to the question that had been running through her mind. "What happened?"

The wind rustled in the trees, threatening to send her question dancing away with the breeze.

Sandrine glanced back at her and grunted. "Answers are given in exchange for answers."

Maeve shrugged. Instead of angering her, Sandrine's taunt was expected. "What do you want to know?" she replied evenly.

Sandrine allowed Maeve to walk alongside her. They were in the flatlands now, without a hill in sight, which made it easier to walk and speak at the same time.

"Who did you see inside the lair?" Sandrine asked matter-of-factly.

Maeve almost paused. *Who*? Did Sandrine know who was in there? Questions raced through her mind and speculation mounted. Was it possible that the scholar, in all her wisdom, knew exactly what situation Maeve had walked into? She swallowed hard, but saw no reason to withhold the truth. "A woman in a golden cage. She had the shard."

"Did she speak to you? Explain her history?" Sandrine asked.

Maeve detected just a hint of something else in Sandrine's tone. Anticipation? Anger? Excitement?

"Aye," Maeve confirmed. "She claimed she was the last of her kind, the sole survivor after the fae invaded Draconbane and killed all the dragons."

"Eh," Sandrine grunted. "Did she speak of her sister?" she asked sharply.

Maeve reached out a hand to touch Sandrine's shoulder. "Sandrine." She searched the scholar's eyes, seeking truth. "What do you know? Why are you asking me these questions when you already know the answers?"

Sandrine stared back boldly, her emotions hidden behind her wrinkled face. "It is a confirmation of the truth, for you have no reason to lie to me."

"Then why do you withhold truth from me?" Maeve's frustration leaked out, and with every word she squeezed Sandrine's shoulder harder. The sorrow ate away at her patience and her anger became impossible to control. "I have asked you time and time again, and it's like a puzzle, but you won't reveal the truth to me until I'm too close to it, and I can't see what this game is. Why Draconbane? Why did you send me in alone? Why didn't you save Caspian? You are a healer, you should have been there. And why are the pirate brothers still alive?"

Sandrine's hand came up so suddenly Maeve almost missed it. A bolt of lightning went through her stomach, and she was hurled backward so violently the breath whooshed out of her. Too startled to respond, she could only glare up at Sandrine in shock. As she did, she realized she'd left a bruise where she'd gripped Sandrine. She felt a sudden urge to scream, tear up trees by their roots, and rip everything apart. But it wouldn't help anything nor solve any problems. Taking a deep breath, she tried to focus on her breathing to calm herself. Stay calm. Ask questions. Discover knowledge. She would not resort to violence again.

"Ask me more," Sandrine demanded, her gray eyes alive with fury. "Ask me why I serve the fae or why I am still alive. Ask me why I warned you against bringing that warlord, or why I gave you the Finder's Stone. Ask. You are a clever girl, strong and clever, and there is a reason you, specifically, were brought on this quest. You were chosen because of who you are. Your heritage. Maeve of Carn. Perhaps it is time to tell you the truth. Perhaps I have spared you long enough. You've begun to suspect, so get up, girl. Stand on your own two feet and accept responsibility for what I am about to reveal to you. When I end my tale, you might wish you had been left in the dark to mope in your frustration. Knowledge is the ultimate source of power, but it is sharper than a double-edged sword. You've faced sorrow, but the knife I plunge into your heart will not be easy to pull out again. Are you sure you want to know?"

Maeve's jaw hung open at the ferocity of Sandrine's words, and she simply lay on the ground, legs spread, staring up at Sandrine.

A warm hand touched her bare arm, and she felt a presence beside her. Imer. "Come on," he persuaded.

Maeve allowed him to guide her to her feet. Then he turned to Sandrine. "We will scout ahead. Call if you need us."

"Go ahead," Sandrine confirmed, jaw set.

Once the two brothers had gone a good bit down the road, Sandrine turned to Maeve. "Well?"

Maeve took a step toward her, breathless. "Tell me," she whispered.

"It all began here, in Draconbane," Sandrine said, her voice taking on a singsong quality. She began to walk, and Maeve fell in stride with her. The wind rushed around them, as though blessing Sandrine's words. "Old tales confirm that this used to be the land of the dragons. Stories often speak of their beast-like appearance, but the dragons were more like us, smart, intelligent, with the ability to shift between a dragon form and a humanlike form. The dragons were ruled by a ruthless king, Belroc, and a cunning queen, Drakaina. Word of their ferocity spread far and wide, so far and wide that the term Draconbane was used, for to awake the dragons meant to invoke the demons, and all who came to this land perished because of the dragons.

"One day, Queen Drakaina had a daughter, named Ariefluer, who became known as the Goblin Queen. The creatures were drawn to her and obeyed her wishes. The Goblin Queen became the pride of the kingdom, for she knew the way of the mind and was a great scholar and strategist. Although the king and queen desired a male heir, the power of their eldest was strong, and thus the kingdom flourished. When the second sister, Drakai, hatched, she did not live up to their expectations. She was not a scholar or strategist, nor did she have the power to read minds. She was, however, known for her quick tongue and violent temperament. Eventually the king and queen died, leaving the sisters to rule Draconbane in their place. There is much speculation about what actually happened to the king and queen; whether they died during a battle or if something happened within the mountains is unknown. It is only said they were killed and given a great burial, and while dragonkind do not live forever, it was known that the king and queen had died young. Too young."

Maeve recalled the flashing eyes of Ariefluer and the cruel smile on her face. Was she the cause of her parents' death, or was it her sister?

"After the king and queen died, Draconbane became wealthy, the capital of the known world. Until the night of the fae. They opened a portal a ten days march away from the city and slipped into Draconbane. Blending into the shadows like they do, they came and destroyed. Legends claim they were after the wealth Draconbane offered. Others claim they were after dragon fire, but either way, they wanted power, and with the corruption of Ariefluer, the Goblin Queen and Drakai, the Dragon Queen, they saw their chance. They took Drakai as a bride for the king of the fae and cursed Ariefluer, but the curse rebounded upon themselves. After their great victory, the fae were banished.

"While there was still awe and fear, freedom gripped the land. Slowly but surely, the legends died away, and the fae became known as nothing more than a terror during the full moon. But the fae found a way. They discovered that wicked people with evil in their hearts and murder in their eyes were easy to pull in to their domain and control. They also found that portals could not be opened everywhere, especially not in holy places. But people were predictable, and the fae found that with promises and threats, people could be controlled and bent to their will. And that is where I come in."

Sandrine trailed off, her eyes vacant, staring ahead.

Maeve stayed silent, giving the scholar space to continue her tale, although her mind whirled with questions. Why did the fae attack Draconbane? It seemed they could have made a deal with the two treacherous queens. It did not add up that the fae would attack the greatest civilization just to secure a bride for their king.

"I killed my husband. Someone I promised to love. Forever." Her words were matter-of-fact, as though she'd relived that moment over and over again, until it had lost its horror and potency. "I had a reputation in my kingdom; I was a healer first and a scholar second. I had a great library full of books I pored over, and some I wrote myself. I knew histories, languages, and lore. I went by many names in that life, and many came to me for wisdom. I had fame, I had everything, until that fateful night. If I had been a commoner, my sins might have been overlooked, but I was in a line of royals—royals who do not forgive or forget. My children were safe, but I was thrown in prison to await execution."

Her hand went to her neck. "They were going to behead me, although hanging is a more common practice now. It just so happened that the night of the full moon came before my execution. The fae came to me and offered me a deal."

Maeve squeezed her hands into fists until her nails bit into the palms of her hands. This was the moment. This was the truth she'd been waiting to hear.

"My heart was full of vengeance and regret, so I took their deal to save my skin. After all, they needed a scholar with skills like mine, to dive into the histories, discover legends, secrets, relics, curses, and so I did. But not because I serve the fae—I care nothing for their kind. I serve the queen, although she is not their queen. She is Drakai, the Dragon Queen, and when the curse is broken, she will be set free."

Maeve's fists came loose although her heart pounded against her skull. This was what she'd feared, and yet also what she'd expected. Someone greater than the fae was behind this, and once she was set free, what would happen? Was she repentant, like her sister? Would she restore Draconbane to its former glory? Or was her heart bent on malice? Would she try to rule the world?

"Why?" Maeve asked, her voice barely above a whisper. "Why do you work for her? What has she promised you? What will you get out of the bargain?"

"It is ironic that you ask that, when you know why you are here, why you still work for the fae, even though you could flee and go where they cannot find you."

"I don't have a choice," Maeve retorted. "They control me; they collared me. If I don't do what they say, I'll never be free."

"Aha." Sandrine jabbed Maeve's arm with a pointed finger. "You long for freedom, which means you will do whatever it takes to restore your freedom—unlike your former friend, the warlord Caspian. He was not like you."

Blood rushed to Maeve's ears. She turned, her heart frozen with terror. Her lips trembled as she spoke the next words, already afraid of what the answer would be. "Speak plainly. What do you mean?"

Sandrine held out a hand and took a step away from Maeve. "Do not take your anger out on me. I had nothing to do with your capture."

"Tell me," Maeve growled, rage boiling in her belly again.

"You were not the first one chosen," Sandrine told her. "It was Caspian. Half a year ago, the fae decided because of his deeds, he would be worthy to take up the quest to find the seven shards. They captured him and made demands, promising to destroy everyone he knew if he did not comply. It started well. He went out on his own, found the first shard, and then hid in a temple. A holy place. The fae could not reach him there, and when he left, he was so changed, they decided to take you instead, because of your heritage.

They decided you would not fail them, not Maeve of Carn."

Tears spilled down Maeve's cheeks. So, Caspian had been trying to save her from the trap he'd fallen into. But she'd fallen nonetheless, and now he was gone, and it was because of their dark deeds that the fae had taken both of them. The darkness in her soul had called out to the fae, and they were able to twist and manipulate her because of it. She turned away from Sandrine, no longer feeling the need to strike her companion. Briefly, she wondered if she, too, could take the shards and hide in a temple until the fae forgot about her.

"What about Carn?" she asked, voice quavering.

"I am old," Sandrine said. "My family has been kept safe because of my service, and yet my grandsons—Ingram and Imer—are blessed with extraordinary powers, which makes them hunted and desired at the same time. I brought them on this quest because I know my time is failing, and you will be safe in their hands. They will take you on to Carn and help you understand. But beware. The next shard lies in Carn, and if anything I have told you has made you unhappy, what you find out there will be devastating."

A rushing came to Maeve's ears as the words, the knowledge, seeped inside, like a river brimming over, filling her, drowning her. She fell to her knees and wrapped her arms around her waist to give herself an anchor, but it wasn't enough.

A sob wrenched itself from her lips and she rocked

back and forth, crying until she had no tears left. Fear, anger, rage, sorrow, and vengeance all twisted in her, emotions so powerful they poured out in a warring cocktail. But when her fingers twisted around her sword hilt, tightening, she knew, beyond a shadow of doubt, that she would stop at nothing until the fae were destroyed.

29

NIGHT OF THE FULL MOON

THE NEXT NINE days passed swiftly, and Maeve looked at her companions with new eyes after Sandrine's revelations. Sandrine the scholar, who had fallen from a house of wealth and wisdom and was using her skills to protect her family, all the way down to her grandchildren. The fae must have had something to do with her mortality, for although she was an older woman, she had not aged as she should have. Meanwhile, the pirate brothers remained the same—they were quiet, kept to themselves, and showed no hints of extraordinary power.

Maeve, lost in her grief, sometimes wondered if she could not see clearly because of her inward focus. Her desire for freedom overwhelmed all other thoughts, but she could sense, even in her desperation, that it was akin to how the fae felt, and how the lost sister of the

Goblin Queen felt. At times she peeked over at Sandrine, wondering about what the woman had said. She had not shared her vision for the future, and had only spoken of what Maeve would discover in Carn. What did it mean? Did Sandrine want her to stop the fae from breaking all curses? Was Sandrine on her side, or was she simply doing what needed to be done to stay alive, to protect her family? Sandrine had answered many questions, and yet created many more, leaving Maeve second-guessing herself.

Each day took them deeper into the land but farther from the Draconbane Mountains. White birds flew ahead, calling out to each other, and the scent of water increased as they moved south. Maeve sensed the change in the richness of the air and the growth of the trees that spread above them, larger than before. They began to see animals again. After the barrenness of Draconbane, it was a relief to see fluffy white bunnies running through the thicket, squirrels chattering as they climbed trees, birds chirping and flirting with each other, and occasionally deer, their eyes wide and solemn as they stood in the shadows, watching invaders trudge through their land. Faintly, old memories began to resurface. Maeve remembered when she was a child running through the woods, shouting and calling out, and then the calm, the quiet, the stealthy movements as she hunted. It all seemed so long ago, before . . .

Maeve opened her eyes. It was late again, and they'd reached a quiet area with woods on one side and a grassy opening on the other, overgrown and sloping downhill.

"It is time," Sandrine said, pointing to the hilltop.

"Time?" Maeve asked.

"It is the night of the full moon," Sandrine said. "Come. We will go to the hilltop and wait for the fae."

Dark visions flashed in Maeve's mind. Her fingers went to the golden collar, thin but strong, holding her captive. She couldn't refuse now; there was nowhere to run, nowhere to hide. Her salvation was the extra shard, but the fae knew that Caspian took one of the seven shards. Would they assume she had picked it up? She hadn't shared the knowledge with Sandrine, out of hope that the fae would assume that the location of the shard died with Caspian.

"I don't have to go with you," Maeve protested. "I can give you the shards, and you can take them to the fae."

Sandrine glowered. "Are you a fool, girl? After all I've told you, don't you understand why the fae are coming here? They need reassurance that you are on their side, that you haven't deviated from the plan and won't go rogue like Caspian did."

Maeve wanted to retort that there was no point, the fae would never trust her, nor would they ever relent.

Shoulders slumped, she followed Sandrine across the plain, heading toward the hilltop. When she glanced back, the brothers had disappeared. "Where are they going?" Maeve kept her voice low.

"I sent them away. They have no business being here." Sandrine shrugged. "After we meet with the fae, take the road south toward Carn. The Finder's Stone will lead you."

The full moon loomed bright in the sky, hovering over the empty glade and illuminating the silver blades of grass and the uncanny emptiness of the field. Maeve stood an arm's length away from Sandrine, arms crossed over her chest, the bag of shards in one hand. At least, two of the shards were in the bag; the other one she'd tucked into her breastplate, where she could feel the cool hardness between her breasts, a reminder to hold firm, hold steady. Too late, she'd thought about hiding the shard elsewhere, or even swallowing it like the Goblin Queen had. But it was too large, and she did not possess the magic necessary to force it down her throat. The Goblin Queen must have been desperate.

The egg was also in her pack, slung over her back along with dried food and waterskins. She doubted the fae would have use for it but all the same, she put the Finder's Stone on top. If asked, she could explain that it was given to her by Sandrine, to help complete the quest. Although she did not understand why Sandrine was leaving her so soon. Hadn't the fae promised her a scholar? Why would they take her away now, after only thirty days when she had another six months before they would demand her debt fulfilled?

A sound whispered through the meadow, followed by a dim roar. Clouds rolled across the sky and a mist with purple swirls filled the air. A hollow whistle sounded and with a sigh the portal opened on the hilltop. It appeared like a storm, a vast whirlpool, and out of it walked four shapes.

Maeve's heart quailed at the sight of them. Reflexively, she straightened her shoulders and set her jaw. She would not be cowed by the fae, not again. A reminder of the dungeon flashed before her eyes. She was upholding her end of the bargain; they needed her, and they would not send her down to the depths again.

When the mist cleared, her heart sank further. The Master was with them, clothed in his dark shroud with the cowl of his cloak pulled low over his head. He'd brought with him the lesser minotaur, who snorted and tapped his javelin against the ground. Surely, he preferred to be at the scene of a battle instead of acting as a guard overseeing the delivery of the shards. With them were two other fae that Maeve did not recognize; tall, stout creatures with gleaming eyes. One had leathery wings folded neatly on its back, reminding Maeve of a demon. Demons were ruthless villains, not unlike the fae. They had a thirst for death, blood, and deception; not that Maeve had ever met a demon, but rumors were enough to confirm the threat.

The Master's dark eyes roved over Maeve, and then

he turned to Sandrine. "Sandrine the scholar, well met. Your presence is requested at court until the next full moon, at which time you will return to this quest. All is in order, I presume."

Sandrine did not cow before him as Maeve expected. She merely fixed him with a look. "I would not be the scholar if it were not as I had said. After you have finished here, I will return with you."

The Master lifted a hand, letting his claws display in the moonlight. A silent threat. "We do not need your presence for this exchange. You will return now."

He waved a hand toward the entrance of the portal.

Sandrine took a step toward it as the purple mist drifted over it. "As you wish," she said, bowing her head. Whether that was a sign of goodwill or submission, Maeve was unsure.

Despite her explanations, Sandrine remained a mystery, and with each step that Sandrine took, a bit of Maeve's hope disappeared. The mist swallowed her whole, and then the portal snapped shut, leaving Maeve alone with the fae.

Suddenly the full moon seemed ominous, and while Maeve knew she simply needed to hand over the shards, she wished the pirate brothers were standing with her. Anything was better than facing the fae alone. Again.

Silence crawled through the glade. Even the wind stilled, cowered into submission. The Master held out his clawed hand. Maeve had to take two steps forward to reach him, stretching out her arm to hand him the bag.

He took it with a mere glance at her and opened it. The two shards gleamed, casting blue shadows across the glade as the Master held them to the moonlight and examined them.

Their beauty struck Maeve. They awoke a longing, deep within, that made her want to reach out and snatch the shards back for herself. Such holy relics did not belong in the hands of the fae. She sucked on her tongue to keep the words that were building in her throat from coming out.

"Two shards," the Master mused as he examined them, "one from the warlord Sebastian. We were there before you, but left it to test you, and you succeeded."

Maeve wasn't sure if there was admiration in his voice, or merely observation.

"One from the lair of dragons, in the Draconbane Mountains. But." His liquid eyes turned on her, so dark and depthless she felt as though she were drowning in them. "Where is the third?"

Maeve's heart froze, but she had expected this. She was ready. "Third? I don't know what you mean—"

The pain came suddenly, a searing agony flaring up her neck, rendering her speechless. The collar around her neck tightened, cutting off her breathing and blurring her vision. Eyes bulging, Maeve gasped, her hands going to her neck, as though she could pry away the collar. It burned her fingers when she touched it, but instead of crying out, only a gurgling sound came from her lips. Her knees gave way, and she fell to the ground, kneeling in front of the Master.

As quickly as it came, the pain faded, leaving her gasping in the grass, eyes wet.

"Restrain her," ordered the Master.

The minotaur pointed his javelin at Maeve while the winged fae and the wingless one came up behind her, ripping her arms from her sides and tying her wrists behind her back. They pulled hard until the rope bit into her hands. Writhing in place, she tried to rise to her feet, but a blow struck the back of her head. Her vision went white and she fell forward, head ringing with pain while they bound her feet. But now the fear was gone, and only fury remained, surging through her. If only she had her strength, she would make them pay, tear their eyes out of their faces and break their limbs. The battle rage rose in her and she struggled, although the bonds were so tight she barely moved.

Then the Master was there, lifting her face by the roots of her hair, forcing her to stare up at him. "Maeve of Carn, you were warned once, do not try my patience again," he snarled, his fangs too close to her face, too near her neck.

"I don't know what you are talking about," Maeve protested. "It's been thirty days; I've only had the chance to gather two shards."

The Master traced a claw from her eye down to her lips, the sharp edge touching but not breaking her skin.

"It is only a warrior's nature; you plot against me, you scheme, but remember who is in control here. Your warlord is dead and he left you his shard. You have chosen not to reveal the location of the shard, and with that choice comes punishment. I will not warn you again."

His claw hovered over her lip, and then with one quick movement, he slashed. Maeve's cry was muffled as her lip split open and blood dripped out.

"Search her," the Master growled, stepping back.

Maeve wanted to speak, to tell him where the shard was, to cave, to give in, but the fire on her mouth would not allow words to come out. She shuddered even as her crown was ripped off her head. The butt of the javelin bit into her side as it pushed her over, and then the fae were upon her. One sat on her legs, ripping off her sandals while the other undid her breastplate, tearing it off, wickedness in his eyes. His tongue came out, forked like a snake's, as he examined her. Maeve was all too aware of the shortness of her shift and then a curved knife came down, ripping open her tunic from the top to her navel. Her bare breasts spilled out, along with the shard. It rolled once it fell into the grass.

The Master snatched it up and then raised his hands, stopping the fae from doing any further damage. He stood in front of Maeve while her shoulders heaved. Her face bloomed with embarrassment and shame. She should have hidden the shard elsewhere, but her anger and grief had made her careless. And now she was truly afraid, laid bare before the fae.

"Disgraceful," the Master snorted. "I had higher hopes for you, Maeve of Carn. The next time you disobey, I will bring the master of the whip with me. He shall enjoy doling out your punishment. This is not over, and I need you prepared to work, but you have shown your aptitude for trickery. Know that your punishment is not your own; the scholar will share in it, and her family."

"Please," Maeve managed to call out, despite the searing pain on her lips. "It was me, only me. The scholar knew nothing. I accept it all."

She didn't know why she was protecting the scholar, but there was something, a reason why she could not let others pay for her sins. Although if it had been thirty days earlier, she wouldn't have said a word.

"Master?" the minotaur asked, a hint of malice and delight in his question as he awaited the bloodletting.

"I shall speak with the scholar, but mark my words, your punishment is only delayed." The Master snapped his fingers.

A cold wind blew on Maeve's bare skin, and mist gathered, creating a portal for the fae to walk through.

"Untie her," the Master ordered the minotaur.

"With pleasure," it snarled.

And then the great hulking beast stood over her, his musk filling the air with a potent, animal odor. He kicked, his hoof smashing into the softness of Maeve's belly. A scream tore out of her lips as her stomach cramped. She writhed in pain, feeling like a gutted fish, still drawing breath with nowhere to go. The collar flared up, burning her neck, shutting down her breathing. She lay gasping as the minotaur cut the binds on her hands, allowing her to curl into a ball to protect herself from any more abuse.

Instead of striking her again, he cut the rope that bound her legs and disappeared into the portal. It closed behind the fae, leaving Maeve bleeding and alone on the hilltop under the light of the full moon.

30

ORC HILL

MAEVE LAY in the grass until she recovered enough to breathe without pain. Although the minotaur hadn't kicked her hard enough to draw blood, she knew she'd have bruises on her stomach in the coming days. She praised the Divine that he hadn't kicked her in the ribs. The intent of the fae was to frighten her, not keep her from completing the quest for them. She sat up to take in her surroundings and reached for her sandals. Some of the straps were torn, but they were still useable. She almost cried when she picked her crown up out of the grass and untangled it from the weeds. Opening her bag, she added the crown to the pile and checked over her things. They were all there, including the Finder's Stone.

She rose with a grunt and lifted first her sword and then her breastplate. The movement caused her stomach to cramp and her lips still burned, but she would not feel sorry for herself, not this time. She turned and saw that down the slope of the hill was a river, wide and shimmering in the moonlight. Glancing around again to ensure she really was alone, she headed toward it.

The riverbank was quiet. One side of the river was open to the field, but the other side, just a short swim away, butted up against the forest. Trees with upright branches and what looked like hair sweeping down toward the water grew there. Weeping willows. A sigh escaped Maeve's parted lips. With trembling fingers, she set down her sandals, bag, breastplate, and sword on a nearby rock. Wiggling out of her torn clothing, she waded into the water. It was cold, and the shock of it almost made her cry out. She wondered if the river came from the snowy mountain peaks, and the run-off of snow kept it cold. The fall weather meant she might catch a chill, but suddenly she wanted nothing more than to be rid of the feeling of the fae holding her arms, kicking her, abusing her. She dived, surrendering to the cold arms of the water. Eyes closed, she let herself drift down, where the water flowed smoothly around her, then pushed herself back toward the surface.

Goosebumps rose on her arm as she floated to the top of the river. Lying on her back, she closed her eyes, allowing the cold to numb her body, numb her senses, and let her forget the predicament she was in. But when she closed her eyes, a vision of Caspian rose before her, his blond head thrown back, laughing as they clinked mugs of ale together, celebrating another great victory. Drunken laughter echoed around them. The memory was from back in the early days, when they sought treasure above all with their rough and tumble crew of motley characters. Adrian, with the scar on his face and dark hair in two braids, was closest to Caspian and handy with a knife. Merloke, a stout man who was always eating. He kept most of his head shaved except for one long braid that went halfway down his back. And Timothy, keeper of the gold, a shrewd man, lean and tall with nimble fingers.

Caspian's hand had rested on her thigh that night—the first time he'd alluded to what was there. Maeve remembered the fire in her belly, the desire for more after a conquest, and yet Caspian had denied her, again and again. It was true he cared for her, but he had never pushed beyond the confines of friendship, of brotherhood.

Tears fell down her face and froze on her cheeks. Now she was alone. Alone in the Draconbane Mountains on a dangerous quest that would destroy the world. Then, suddenly, she was rushing out of the water to the shallows and kneeling in the mud. Stones poked at her, but she folded her hands, bowed her head, closed her eyes, and prayed under the moonlight.

Oh, Divine One.

Grant me mercy.

If you listen to the cries of those below you.

There's nothing left for me here.

I don't see a way out of this.

Every action I take hurts another.

I need relief.

I need mercy.

I crave forgiveness.

Show me a new path.

Show me a way.

Help me stop this madness.

Halt the rise of the fae.

When she lifted her head, ice-cold hair brushing down her back, she saw a stag upon a hilltop with antlers that pointed upward toward the heavens, but it was white as the feather she'd found during her first week in Draconbane. A rarity. A sign. She pressed her hand to her heart in acknowledgement. The pain in her chest, the frightened desperation, faded away, and peace—a peace she could not understand nor comprehend—swept through her, as though a presence filled her. Although she was still in the same predicament and no flashes of light had come from the sky, she felt something shift. She rose to her feet and iron determination rose in her core.

She had nothing to lose—aside from her life—and everything to gain from taking down the fae. Throughout her warring career she'd risked other lives, and now the stag seemed to agree, it was time for her to face the consequences of her actions and risk her own life. It's what she wanted, but more importantly, it was what Caspian would have wanted. Something noble.

A slight wind blew as she stood there, naked, and then a chill swept over her body. A cold warning. Shivering, she reached for her tunic and whatever spell lay over the hillside snapped.

Run.

The voice seemed to be in her head, and she glanced up toward the stag. Its dark eyes peered at her, and then it turned and started running south. But the voice—where had it come from? Why was it in her head?

With shaking fingers, Maeve dragged her torn shift over her head. Her stomach protested when she reached for her breastplate, but she pulled it on with some difficulty, her cold fingers hindering her progress. As she dressed, she heard a snapping sound and then muffled grunts. Snatching up her sandals, she wrapped the torn leather around her legs, willing herself to move faster. Something was out there; it would take too long to pause and look around, but it sounded like it was coming from the other side of the river, in the dense woods where she could not see. And she was standing there in the moonlight, a clear target for any arrows. Her tongue went dry. Her hand wrapped around the hilt of her blade and tugged it free of the scabbard, then she tossed her bag on her back and began to run alongside the riverbank. South. It was difficult to hit a moving target, and she hoped she was moving too quickly for whatever was out there.

Her mind raced, and although she knew it was unlikely goblins were around, there were many foul creatures that called Draconbane home, and she was alone. A curse passed over her torn lip, but the numbness of the water had not worn off yet and the fire building in her belly kept the pain at bay.

The grunt came again, followed by a loud snort. Maeve heard footsteps, and although she knew her focus should be solely on running, she wanted to know what was chasing her, so she glanced back. There were two creatures running on the opposite side of the bank. They were big, taller than her, and bulky, more brute strength than anything else. They were dressed in rags with gray skin and bloated, ugly faces. Her heart pounded in her throat. Orcs. By the Divine. Orcs were chasing her. But there were only two; she could take them.

Her foot snagged on a root and she went down hard, catching herself with one hand while her sword went flying, landing a few feet in front of her. Maeve scrambled to her knees just as the bulk of something slammed into her side, bowling her over. Lashing out, Maeve kicked and scratched at the creature. Rough black hair came away in her hand and a sour stink—like rotten eggs left out in hot sunlight—filled her nostrils. Bile rose in her throat as she scrambled toward her sword, but the creature was not far behind her. It snatched at her hair, forcing a cry of frustration from her lips. In her haste, she hadn't braided her hair nor tossed it on top of her head. Now, free and wild, it was a danger to her. She hooked an elbow back, hoping to catch the creature in the eye, but the fist holding her hair was strong and did not let go. Something warm moved over her legs, holding them down, pressing her into the mud.

Maeve wiggled in frustration and stretched out her arms. Her fingers grazed the hilt of her sword and she struggled under the weight of the creature, determined to reach her blade. The hand pulled on her hair, dragging her head back. Legs kicking feebly, Maeve realized its intention. The creature meant to bare her neck and slit her throat, leaving her blood to drain out by the riverside. She struggled as the weight pressed down, tears leaking out of her eyes from the pain in her skull. Oh, Divine One, not like this. She couldn't die facedown in the mud, attacked by orcs because she forgot to watch her back.

Rearing back in frustration, a cry of rage poured out of the pit of her being. Startled by her movement, the creature lost its tight grip, and that was all Maeve needed. She snapped her head back, her skull colliding with the hard face of the creature. It grunted and let go of her completely, giving her the leverage she needed to reach her sword. Her fingers closed around the blade and she twisted around, screaming as the movement wrenched her bruised stomach, for her legs were still held fast by the creature. She came face to face with the orc sitting on her and slashed at it. The creature rolled off her, holding its cheek and wailing.

The knife it carried dropped to the ground and Maeve snatched it up in her free hand. First, she rose to her knees, then she gingerly stood up on her feet and glanced around. The other two orcs were midway across the river, roaring as they pointed their blades at her. A knife whirled past her arm, clanged against her breastplate, and bounced off. Checking to ensure her bag was still on her back, Maeve took off, running uphill, desperate to leave the orcs behind.

Shadows rose and fell on the grass, and the moonlight was not bright enough to light her path. Twice she stumbled and almost fell while the orcs came on, grunting, their breathing loud and coarse. Maeve didn't know where she was going, other than south, and she was unsure where she should hide. Eventually she'd become winded and have to stop, and while she didn't know if there were more orcs in the area, she did know the ones following her would alert any others if there were.

Her breath came short and fast. Before the fae, she'd been able to run and fight almost indefinitely, but the collar lay heavy around her neck, sapping her extraordinary strength away. Oh, how she hated the fae for what they'd done to her. Emotions tumbled through her; rage, anger, grief, and then guilt. They came in waves, but it was the guilt that overwhelmed her as she dashed through the long grass, legs burning as she gained the hillside and followed the slope back down. The river disappeared, hidden behind more hills, and the forest loomed ahead, thick, wooded, covered. A shelter. Her heart pumped hard and fast in her chest, blood rose in her throat, and her sides ached, crying out for relief, especially after the beating she'd taken earlier. The grunts of the orcs came closer; they were gaining on her, their legs fast, built for speeding over the hilly terrain.

The trees rose in front of Maeve and she stopped, ready to make her last stand. Twirling the sword and the stolen knife in her hands, she spun to face the orcs, and to the surprise of both, dashed straight toward them, blades out. The orcs paused, only for a moment, but it was enough. Maeve whirled past them, lashing out with her blades and striking true. She heard them roar as the blades found flesh and there came a ripping, tearing sound. Grim satisfaction rolled through her as she spun around and dashed back toward them. This time the orcs were ready, although black blood rolled down one's shoulder. Baring rotten teeth at her, they charged, blades swinging.

Before she were collared, she wouldn't have worried about taking down two orcs at once, but it took all of her wits to duck, bob, and weave between the two creatures, trading blows with them. They were both strong, and despite their bulk, fast. Maeve's heart quailed as she fought, giving up ground as the two orcs edged in on her, blades whirling, tongues out as they saw their kill.

A blade cut across her forearm and she hissed, fire raging in her belly. She struck out with the knife, catching the first orc in the neck. It roared in surprise and anguish, both hands going to its neck where black blood spurted out. The other orc roared at the loss of its comrade, but Maeve stayed patient, blocking its blows —which came with increased fury—until it made a mistake and Maeve saw her chance. She brought her blade crashing down on its arm, which came off, leaving the orc howling. The creature dropped its blade and charged her, splurging blood across her breastplate. Maeve kicked out, knocking it back, and then swung her sword with pleasure, bringing the blade straight down into its heart. There was a sickening crunch and then the orc lay still. Breathing hard, Maeve wiped her sword on its clothes and stood tall, chest heaving as she caught her breath.

A sound made her turn and take another gasping breath. On the hilltop, dark shapes were gathering. Orcs.

31

GOBLIN QUEEN'S GIFT

Maeve bolted into the sparse wood, using the muted light of the moon to guide her way as she dashed, heart pounding in her throat. Pain from fighting the orcs faded away, leaving only the maddening sense that she had to escape, to outrun the horde of orcs that were coming for her. All reasoning fled and bitterly she considered whether the fae had alerted the orcs to her location just to toy with her. But why would the fae continue to plague her when she was working for them and doing her best to find the shards within the time limit they had set? It was madness to assume they also wanted her dead. But did they? Was there someone else they could use to find the shards? Or was Sandrine correct? Did they really need her, specifically, to complete the quest?

A tree branch whipped across her face, the sharp

ends slapping against her bruised lip. Belatedly, Maeve cried out and raised a hand to shield her face. The next moment she almost cursed at her mistake. Surely the orcs had heard her, and now knew where she was in the wood. Setting her jaw, she shoved the pain to the back of her mind and pushed on.

She wasn't sure what time it was when the trees thinned and opened up to a glade. She glanced back, but it was too dark to see in the wood. When she looked up, she noted that clouds were gathering across the sky, clouds that would hide the moon and momentarily give her shelter. Squaring her shoulders, Maeve took a deep breath and started across the glade, running as fast as she could, sword in hand in case any creature threatened her during her mad flight. Instead, she felt something move, something on her back, and a distinct cracking sound came to her ears.

The egg! But not here. Not right now, in the middle of her flight. She did not have the time to stop and deal with whatever was in that egg. Her stomach twisted with horror at the thought of what it could be. Spawn of the Goblin Queen; what did it mean? What was the true nature of the Goblin Queen? A goblin, a human, a mage, a dragon, or something else?

A second crack came to her ears, and the bag on her back shook. Curses came to Maeve's mind, but she kept moving, determined to reach the shelter of the trees. Then a pain seized one of her legs. Maeve went down hard, holding out her hands to keep herself from smashing her face on the ground. A low whistling sound came and Maeve saw an arrow whoosh a few inches over her head. Eyes wide, she began to crawl on her elbows and knees, staying low in case more arrows came.

How foolish of her. She should have kept to the trees instead of dashing across the glade. She didn't know the terrain nor where the orcs held camp. What if she were dashing into their midst? She'd blindly assumed the orcs at the river had come from a camp and were perhaps scouting, but now she realized her lack of knowledge could be her death. When she fought with Caspian, they always had scouts to go through an area first, report back on stations, changing of the guards, and all other details that might prove useful. But out here, she was in wild lands where dangerous creatures roamed. Alone. It was hard not to consider the fact that the fae had set her up for this. Perhaps they truly were finished with her, and an ambush by orcs was how they meant to get rid of her. Although it would have been much faster for the minotaur to slit her throat.

But there had been that moment by the riverside when peace invaded her being, peace she'd only felt one other time, and that was when she prayed to the Divine. It was a sign that there was a way out of this situation; she just had to be mindful. Resolve swept through her. Gritting her teeth, she crawled faster, trying to ignore the whistles of more arrows and the grunts as creatures came out of hiding spots, dashing to where she'd gone down. They must have thought they'd gotten her and the trees were close, oh so close.

A high-pitched shriek came from her bag and then it began to wiggle in earnest, as though there were a creature in it, fighting for escape. The spawn of the Goblin Queen had birthed, and it was loose in her bag. A real fear settled in the pit of Maeve's stomach. What was the creature in her bag? Although it was small and newborn, she could only assume it was something dark, something dangerous. She crawled faster, curious to see what it was, and yet dreading the fact. For all she knew, she could be carrying a demon in her bag, and its cries were drawing the orcs.

As soon as Maeve reached the line of trees, it seemed as though her bag came alive. The cries of the creature inside reached a new pitch as it fought to escape. The sounds were like the cry of a baby bird, high and wild and insistent, demanding nourishment. Maeve flung the bag off her back and set it gently on the ground, watching it move under the weight of the creature. Behind her, she knew the orcs snuck closer, and the clouds were nearly done passing over the moon; soon it would be light again, and while she needed to run on, her breathing was becoming labored, and she knew she needed to slow down, regain her breath, figure out what was in her bag, and get ready to fight again, if necessary.

Holding her sword in one hand, she tipped her bag on its side and opened it. Then she stepped back, eyes narrowed, and waited to see what would come out. The fury of shrieking calmed down as the creature found the opening. It gave a little cry, and then Maeve saw a long snout peek out. She held her breath; it was hard to see in the low light, but out came clawed feet, sharp like a cat's, and then a body that looked like it was covered in a tough hide, scaly and long with an almost orange sheen to it. Maeve gasped when she saw the thin layer of skin on its back in the shape of . . . wings? Were those wings? It was difficult to tell, but from everything she'd ever heard, it seemed she looked on a baby dragon.

Her fingers tightened on her sword hilt as decisions warred within her. Witnessing the birth of a dragon was a miracle, and yet the beast was dangerous. It should be killed before it could become like the others, an abomination. What if it was like the Goblin Queen? One who held magical power? Would it shift and take on human form? Aside from what Sandrine had told her, she did not know much about dragons, and what she'd learned led her to believe they were greedy, evil conquerors. She should probably kill it, and yet she longed to know more. A dragon. She had a dragon! What if it grew? What if it could be controlled? What if she could use it against the fae?

There was a snarl, and she realized the orcs were still coming. If she were smart, she would cut off the head of the dragon and run on. Taking a step toward it, she lifted her blade. Golden eyes stared back at her, unblinking. There was something within them that gave Maeve pause. Uttering a cry of frustration, she reached out a hand toward the creature. It was a newborn, and she'd hastily promised the Goblin Queen to take care of whatever was inside the egg. If it proved to be a threat, she would kill it later.

The dragon took a step and sniffed her fingers. Its tongue came out, warm and coarse, and licked her hand. Then it looked up at her and squawked. Maeve almost laughed. Gently, she reached for her bag and turned it over. A liquid poured out of it, hot and hissing. Egg shells drifted out along with a sour smell; the stink of birth.

Maeve groaned. The waterskins were okay, but the dried meat was soured. Quick as a flash, the dragon leaned forward and snapped up a piece of dried meat, then spit it out and squawked in Maeve's direction. As soon as she shook off the orcs, she needed to hunt both for herself and the little beast. Still questioning her decision, she reached for it, fingers closing around the scaly body. The scales almost bit into her, but ignoring that, she lifted the lizard-like creature to her shoulder, glanced back toward the glade, and set off deeper into the forest. The dragon gave one last squawk and then fell silent as they ran, as though it knew of the danger.

The trees grew close together, and there were dense bushes and undergrowth, making Maeve stumble as she fought her way through. The trees rose uphill and inclined sharply in places. But just when she thought she was rid of the orcs, she came to the crest of a hill that dropped away into an orc camp. Cursing her luck, she backed away, wondering how she'd missed the smell of campfires or the yellow light shining off the various structures and tents where the orcs lived. Several were patrolling the area, and she saw some butchering carcasses of dead animals. There was a scent of blood in the air, and Maeve desperately hoped the dragon would not give them away. If it opened its mouth, she would kill it.

Taking a deep breath, she began to back away, determined to skirt around the edge of the camp and make her way off into the forest, all the while hoping against hope that she would not meet any scouts along the way.

"Maeve." The whispered word invaded her ears, and she startled, upsetting the dragon.

32

INTO THE WOOD

THE DRAGON'S claws dug into her shoulder, making her wince. She turned toward the voice and a volley of emotions rose at who she saw. Imer crouched mere paces away from her, his dark clothes blending into the ever-changing shadows of the forest. He lifted a hand and put a finger to his lips before motioning for Maeve to join him.

Maeve's fists clenched tight, and she was unsure whether she felt relief or anger. A warning twisted through her gut, and as much as she wanted—desired—Imer, she was left with an odd sensation when it came to the brothers. Could she trust them? They worked with Sandrine, and ever since the scholar had disappeared through the portal, Maeve had been fighting off a sinking, queasy feeling. Caspian, the only person she truly trusted, was dead, and his death had revealed an ugly secret. He'd had his reasons, but there was no getting around the fact that he'd hidden a shard from her. But right now, it was the orcs or the brothers, and the brothers were the lesser of the two evils. She took a step toward Imer and the dragon squawked.

A curse rose to Maeve's lips, and she froze, glancing down at the encampment. The orcs continued about their nightly duties; some had paused to look up, but most kept working, skinning animals and cutting off chunks of meat. It was likely they were used to odd sounds in the night. Swallowing hard, Maeve inched her way toward Imer, who rose, standing tall and squinting as he looked at the creature on her shoulder.

He shrugged and then said, "Follow me." He turned, silent as the shadows, and slipped through them.

Maeve followed, relieved she had a companion, even if she didn't fully trust him.

They rushed through the trees, Imer setting a quick pace. Maeve managed to keep up, although her leg burned and she felt warm liquid running down to pool in her sandals. When Imer stopped, Maeve felt lightheaded and dizzy. The dragon clung to her, whimpering in her ear, and she knew its claws had pierced her skin for she felt the blood dripping down her back.

"Come, Maeve," Imer said at just above a whisper. "Rest here for a time."

"Did you find her?" a low voice called. Ingram. He carried a blue light as he walked out of what looked like a tunnel. The trees were dense at the top but wider near the bottom, creating a strange sort of enclosure. It was much darker here, as they were in an area the moonlight could not penetrate.

"Aye, wandering near the orc camps. She has a creature with her, I think it might be hungry."

Ingram grunted in response, but Maeve did not see where he disappeared to. She reached out a hand for a tree, suddenly feeling as though she would vomit.

"Wounded, eh?" came Imer's gentle voice. "Here. Sit, catch your breath. I don't think we were followed."

Maeve sank to the ground. It was cool and hard, but it was a relief to be off her aching feet. She sensed the dragon leave her shoulder, claws wrenching out, leaving her flesh punctured and broken.

There was a clicking sound, and she opened one eye to see Imer holding out strips of fresh meat to the baby dragon. It crawled toward him, snatching up the meat in its powerful jaws.

"By the gods, is that a dragon?" Ingram's deep voice came.

"I believe so," Imer agreed. "Odd, isn't it? But we are in Draconbane."

Ingram swore. "It's as the prophecy foretold, isn't it?"

Silence reigned as the brothers watched the dragon eat. "She looks bad. You should tend to her wounds," Ingram suggested. "I'll keep watch."

"Take the dragon with you, will you?" Imer asked.

Maeve closed her eyes again, listening to the low

murmurs. Somewhere, she heard the nocturnal creatures of the wood rustling through the thicket, calling to each other with snarls and sharp barks. An owl hooted, a mouse screamed, and the cycle of life continued. Maeve took a deep breath, her feelings aligning with the mouse. She felt as though she'd been caught in the claws of a predator and escaped, but just for a little while. All too soon a reckoning would come, and she did not see a way out. Not yet.

"Maeve." A presence came near, and a hand lifted her head. "Drink this."

Maeve opened her eyes. There was a blueish light, like the jellyfish lights they'd kept in their ship, *Lucky Jane*. Imer hovered over her, and again she was struck by the gold flakes in his eyes, and the compassion she saw there. Was she wrong to feel the way she felt? The connection to him, the longing? All resistance faded away when he touched her. Was he blessed with a spell to make her forget her wits?

"I know it hurts," he went on, lifting a cup to her lips, "but this will help."

Her eyes narrowed just the slightest bit; what did he know about pain? But she lifted her head all the same, parted her torn lips, and drank, blinking to keep the agony at bay. The substance was warm and slipped down her throat, numbing the pain.

"I'm not the kind of healer Sandrine is," Imer admitted, though his voice seemed far away, "but I do know a thing or two."

Something touched her lip, a kind of paste. She pressed her lips together and earned a chuckle from Imer. "Don't eat it though, it won't taste too good."

She tried to smile at him; why was she smiling when she was exhausted? And where was the dragon? What was Ingram doing with it? "The dragon?" she whispered.

"We will take care of it, my fair lady," Imer quipped. He moved down to her legs and deftly removed the sandals, then began cleaning her wound. "You should rest so we can travel on tomorrow. You got lucky; the arrow barely nicked you. If it had gone straight through, you might have been out of a leg for life." He gave a wry chuckle, but Maeve closed her eyes, unused to his jesting.

As though sensing her attitude, Imer continued to work in silence, binding her leg just below the knee, where the arrow had bitten off a chunk of flesh. He moved around to her shoulder where the dragon had sat, tsking as he applied a paste. "My lady, it would be better not to carry a dragon on your shoulder until you have a perch for it. I had a friend who had a hawk, a common practice among lords who hunt. I will make something similar for your dragon friend once we leave this place."

His fingers went to her breastplate, rolling her onto her side so he could undo it. Maeve reached up, placing her fingers on his wrist. His body was warm, almost hot to the touch, and she wondered at the heat he gave off.

What was the power Sandrine had spoken of? She'd seen no clear signs of it. "Why are you doing this?" she asked.

She caught the cocky smile, the mask he hid behind. "A beautiful woman in need of my skills? How could I resist?"

"No." Maeve held on tighter. "Why?"

The smile fell away and his dark eyes grew somber. "Some evils should not exist," he whispered. "I've studied the scrolls, the prophecies of old, the legend of the fae, of dragons, and of celestials. I sense a change is coming, but it all began with Carn. You have to go back, go back to your roots, and find what was hidden there."

"Carn," she whispered, and she closed her eyes, shutting out Imer's questioning look.

What was in Carn? What memories had she repressed all these years? She remembered her homeland in flashes, and yet she couldn't help but sense that the vision she'd seen in the Sea of Sorrows was somehow connected. The woman screaming, the child being stabbed to death, and the world burning, burning, burning around her.

"Rest, Maeve," Imer murmured. "We'll talk during sunrise."

33

FAE UNDERGROUND

To her credit, Sandrine the scholar showed no fear, nor remorse. She stood with her arms crossed around the book she carried everywhere with her and her pack still slung over her back. Mrithun watched her calmly, clicking his claws, debating whether he should punish her. They were alone in a small chamber that contained books and scrolls. It was where Sandrine went about her work, and where Mrithun and Drakai watched over her, ready to pore over every scroll and book she found. Often, she requested raids on cities with libraries, and although many old scrolls and books were stored in holy places, the fae had their way of manipulating others to do their bidding. Thus, the library had grown, the knowledge of the seven shards had fallen into the hands of the fae, and Drakai had taken a keen interest in learning from Sandrine. In part, the reason Mrithun wanted to punish the scholar was because of Drakai. The two had become close, and at times he suspected they planned without him, telling him only what they wanted him to know. Alas he had no proof, but if and when he got any, his fury would know no bounds.

His thoughts changed as Drakai walked into the room. She wore a sheer gown, and her long hair tumbled around her folded wings. She glided through the doorway like a beast of the night, her eyes alighting only on Sandrine. "Sit," she encouraged the scholar, "tell us what happened."

"All goes according to plan." Sandrine sniffed. Her voice never failed to be grumpy, as though she were displeased at the life she'd been fated to live.

Drakai shook back her hair, and her honey-colored eyes flickered with interest. "Tell me about the warrior. Maeve of Carn. Will she be a problem for us?"

Mrithun waved his claws in dismissal. "She is controlled through the collar, my angel. You need not concern yourself with her."

Drakai tilted her head, eyeing Mrithun with displeasure. "I asked the scholar. I am well aware of what you have done, but you used dark magic, and perhaps a curse, to collar her. I need to know if she can be turned, if she will be on our side when the curse if broken. For if we are free, she will be too, and she could be our greatest ally or fiercest enemy. I know she is a Carnite, perhaps the last one."

"She will not be turned," Sandrine spoke quickly and clearly. "Her mind is made up to betray you and escape as soon as she can. It would not surprise me if she went to hide in a holy place."

Drakai held Mrithun's gaze a moment longer, and then a wicked smile made her lips curve up. She barred her teeth and then addressed Sandrine. "But your grandsons will ensure she does not."

"They will go to Carn," Sandrine said, "which will be emotional for her. My grandsons will be there to comfort her."

"Comfort," Drakai purred. "Now you see, Mrithun? When a woman is in trouble, she cannot help but fall for a man who is there to assist her. So it shall be with Maeve of Carn. You may bully her if you wish, but she is a warrior—she can take it. The greater evil is for her to fall in love with someone who is not who she thinks they are."

Mrithun scoffed. "How do you know that she will not persuade them to join her?"

"Because of the Prophecy of Erinyes," Sandrine spoke up, lifting her chin. "More than anything, they want it to come true. But when the Seven Shards are put back together, chaos will reign, and the land will become a bloodbath. So prepare your armies; prepare for the worst."

"A bloodbath." Drakai grinned and a light came to her eyes. She rose to her feet, stretching out her golden wings. They were thick, leathery, and did not stretch out all the way before she folded them on her back again. "I am ready, the sword is ready. Let chaos descend."

34

BROTHERS OF FIRE

NIGHTMARES PLAGUED MAEVE'S REST. She dreamed of the woman screaming after the child, and then the fire morphed and shifted, shooting out of the mountains and the goblins poured forth, screaming and running from the fire. The fae rose, tall as giants, their impossible figures blotting out the sky while full-grown lizard-like creatures—dragons—roared behind them, ripping up mountains and tearing about the skies.

A scream tore out of Maeve's mouth as she sat up. Sweat rolled down her neck and her breastplate slipped, sliding off her torso. But someone thoughtful had placed a blanket over her and she snatched at it, grateful for something to hold on to.

Looking around, she realized she was not quite alone in the room. Beside her slept the dragon, curled up with its tail next to its head. Reaching out a finger, she stroked its head, marveling at the smoothness of the scales. Despite the ferocity of the creature and the future devastation it could wreak, she felt drawn to its wild, animalistic nature. She wondered if she should name it. It's what others did with the creatures they kept, horses, hawks, sometimes stray dogs even. But perhaps it was best not to get attached.

Close to the dragon was food and a waterskin. Unconcerned about modesty, Maeve reached out, suddenly realizing how hungry she was. Her lip protested slightly when she opened her mouth, but the paste Imer had put on her wounds had seemed to take away all pain. Perhaps he was a healer after all.

As she ate, she studied her surroundings, taking in the way the trees pressed close together and let in only a little light from the sunrise. A glimmer of pink showed through the trees, a bloodred morning, and she shivered at the thought. There were shadows near the entrance to the grove of trees, shadows she assumed were Imer and Ingram, keeping watch while she slept. She wondered if they'd taken turns throughout the night checking on her and ensuring the orcs stayed far away. A spark of gratitude filled her heart, and for a moment she was taken aback at her reaction.

After eating, she put her breastplate back on and reached for her sword. Blood had ruined her shoes, but her feet were tough and she was sure something makeshift could be found in the surrounding wood. Eventually, she'd need to find new clothes that weren't ripped and bloody. She was running her fingers through her tangled hair, trying to make sense of it, when a shadow grew larger and Imer walked into the enclosure.

His brows lifted, a question in his eyes as he glanced to where the food had been and the sleeping dragon. "My lady, how are your wounds?" he asked gently.

Heat flared in her cheeks and, letting go of her tangled hair, she dropped her hands to her sides. She'd never been shy, but Imer's presence made her feel something different; not shyness, but a desire to please. His taking an interest in her made her want to hold it, keep it. Besides, he'd seen her wounded, vulnerable, and instead of taking advantage, he'd helped her. She rubbed her hands on her thighs and then sat on the makeshift bed. "Much better, thank you. You are a healer, aren't you?"

"Yes and no." He shrugged, moving closer to her. "I used rare herbs, as healing power does not come naturally to me."

Maeve raised her head to study him. "But you have innate powers, don't you?"

His smile froze on his lips, and a hint of darkness flashed through his eyes, so quick that Maeve almost didn't see it. "What makes you say that?"

Now it was Maeve's turn to shrug. "I sense it. Besides, Sandrine . . . er . . . the scholar mentioned it."

Imer's lips thinned and then he sat down, crossing his legs in front of her. "That she did. Listen, Maeve, there are many things we don't know about each other. I must admit, I wasn't prepared to care until I learned you are of Carn. But now I've seen you fight, lose someone you cared deeply about, and still, your determination drives you. I am not asking for trust, only a bargain. Ingram and I are in a bit of trouble, so when Sandrine asked us to join this quest, even though it's through these wild lands, we agreed. It's important we lie low for a time and stay away from crowded cities. When Sandrine told us where we were going, I must admit, I became interested. I've wanted to return to the ruins of Carn, where I understand the next shard is hidden, for years; but it lies through orc land, as you have seen for yourself."

He dropped his eyes, gazing at the ground as though it would give him answers. His focus shifted to the slumbering dragon, and a light came to his eyes. "Regardless, traveling with you has been an adventure. There are dragons again, and the time is coming when the prophecy will come true. Will you come with us to Carn?"

City of ruins. Thoughts of Carn flitted through her memory and her fingers shook. She was afraid. Why was she afraid? She took a deep breath, wondering if she should trust the brothers, but after all she had learned, there seemed no other option. She leaned forward and felt the heat from his body. A tingling sensation started at her fingertips and wormed its way through her. His scent floated to her, warm, like a fire on a cold day, a beacon of hope. He held out a hand, reaching up to cup her cheek, and she did not slap his hand away. Instead, she leaned in to his touch and closed her eyes, feeling the smoothness of his fingers, the warmth in his hand, as though a fire simmered within him.

"I will come with you," she whispered, opening her eyes to meet his. "No other option lies before me, and I've lost everything."

There was sympathy in his dark eyes, and understanding. He brushed her cheek with his thumb, a soothing motion that made her heartbeat quicken. "Losing everything does not mean the end. I think going back to the beginning will reveal the key to your freedom, what you have been missing."

"But why? And what about the Prophecy of Erinyes? What do you know about it?" She studied his face, as though it would give her answers, his high cheekbones, the impudent twist of his mouth, his deep-set eyes, and his thick hair, neatly brushed back from his forehead, as though he'd taken the time that morning to work on his appearance.

He moved closer to her, dropping his voice. "The Carnites were the protectors, the last defenders of kingdoms. They were not human; they were a mix between celestials and human, born to guard our world. According to the Prophecy of Erinyes, when Carn was destroyed, the last defender would have the chance to save the world from those below and those above. When I learned of Sandrine, I looked into the lore of the world. You have a chance to become the last defender, but only if you remember what happened in Carn and take up the power that still rests there."

Maeve stopped short of biting her lip and reopening her wound. Disappointment swelled in her breast. "So, you want something from me too. They all do." She turned away and his fingers shifted, slipping down to brush her neck. "I am not a protector, defender, or hero, I just want to be free."

"There will be no freedom if the world is in bondage," Imer countered, "and you are not alone, not anymore."

He let go of her and rose to his feet, shaking back his thick hair as he did. His ears sprang up and out, pointed ears, unnaturally large.

Maeve gasped. No wonder he wore the hat and kept his hair over his ears. He wasn't human either. He was . . . no. He couldn't be, and yet there was no other explanation. But how? How did it happen? How was he walking in daylight if he was fae? She scooted back, scooted away from him, but he wasn't done yet. With a snap of his fingers, his hand burst into flames and his skin glowed.

Understanding washed over Maeve, but she could do nothing but stare at him, heart pounding in her throat. Fire. The goblins had burned; that's how they'd escaped. She didn't know whether to laugh or cry; surely the Divine was toying with her. She'd been fighting so hard to escape the fae, and yet she'd ended up with fae brothers after all. Is this what the king of the fae intended? Did he and Sandrine manipulate her into joining with the brothers on purpose?

Imer waved his hand and the fire disappeared, leaving white smoke drifting off his fingertips, his hand just as smooth as before. A rogue smile came to his features, and then he saw the horror on Maeve's face. Instantly he was beside her, kneeling in front of her, his heat almost unbearable. "It's not what you think, Maeve of Carn. We may have fae blood, but it is not born of darkness and evil deeds. We were born of love and light, to defeat the dark fae. That is our course, and now you know our secret. We are the brothers of fire. Whether or not you want to come with us is still up to you. But, like I said, you are not alone anymore."

"It's all too much," Maeve gasped. "I don't understand."

He nodded as he took her hands in his. "You don't have to. You just need a bit of faith."

Faith. The sentiment rang a bell. Caspian had reminded her, many times, about faith. She had to find a cause, a quest, a reason to be noble. She thought back to his death, his desire, and the secrets he'd kept, perhaps to save her, although it had done nothing good. What would Caspian want from her now? But she knew, even before she opened her mouth, she would go with the brothers of fire. She would walk with them to Carn, and understand her past, her heritage. And then together, they would work to stop the fae.

Tears swam in her eyes for a moment. She would stay on guard, stay wary of the brothers and their true motives. They were dangerous, but if they could help her, she needed to take a risk and learn how to trust again. She squeezed Imer's hands and looked him in the eyes, noting the hints of gold, fire, that danced there.

"Aye. I'll come with you."

Dear Readers,

Thank you for reading *Pawn.*

If you enjoyed the tale and have a few minutes to spare, it would make my day if you would leave a brief review on the site where you bought the book. Just a few words on what you thought about Maeve, the seven shards, and the fate of the world would be perfect.

Leave a Review on Amazon

Maeve of Carn will return in the following books:

Fated

Noble

ACKNOWLEDGMENTS

A special thanks goes out to:

My husband for encouraging my work and providing me with plenty of creative inspiration.

Courtney Andersson for amazing edits and going above and beyond to make this story come alive.

Raquel A. Beattie for recording the audiobook and bringing the characters to life.

Readers far and wide who enjoy these kinds of stories and send kind words and notes. I'm always happy to hear from fans. I truly hope you enjoyed this tale and are looking forward to the many fantastical stories to come.

ALSO BY ANGELA J. FORD

Join my email list for updates, previews, giveaways, and new release notifications. Join now: www.angelajford.com/signup

The Four Worlds Series

A complete 4-book epic fantasy series spanning 200 years, featuring an epic battle between mortals and immortals.

Legend of the Nameless One Series

A 5-book epic fantasy adventure series featuring an enchantress, a wizard and a sarcastic dragon.

Night of the Dark Fae Trilogy

A complete epic fantasy trilogy featuring a strong heroine, dark fae, orcs, goblins, dragons, anti-heroes, magic and romance.

Tales of the Enchanted Wildwood

Adult fairy tales blending fantasy action-adventure with steamy

romance. Each short story can be read as a stand-alone and features a different couple.

Tower Knights

Gothic-inspired adult steamy fantasy romance. Each novel can be read as a stand-alone and features a different couple.

Gods & Goddesses of Labraid

A warrior princess with a dire future embarks on a perilous quest to regain her fallen kingdom.

Lore of Nomadia Trilogy

The story of an alluring nymph, a curious librarian, a renowned hunter and a mad sorceress as they seek to save—or destroy—the empire of Nomadia.

ABOUT THE AUTHOR

Angela J. Ford is a bestselling author who writes epic fantasy and steamy fantasy romance with vivid worlds, gray characters and endings you just can't guess. She has written and published over 20 books.

She enjoys traveling, hiking, and playing World of Warcraft with her husband. First and foremost, Angela is a reader and can often be found with her nose in a book.

Aside from writing she enjoys the challenge of working with marketing technology and builds websites for authors.

If you happen to be in Nashville, you'll most likely find her enjoying a white chocolate mocha and daydreaming about her next book.

facebook.com/angelajfordauthor
twitter.com/aford21
instagram.com/aford21
amazon.com/Angela-J-Ford/e/B0052U9PZO
bookbub.com/authors/angela-j-ford

Made in the USA
Columbia, SC
02 April 2022

58412236R00181